VOW

1/2986 - Book 4

ANNELIE WENDEBERG

All you need to know...

Find me and my books here:
www.anneliewendeberg.com

to
those
who
resist

Part One

_____

The society that separates its scholars from its warriors will have its thinking done by cowards and its fighting done by fools.

Thucydides

One

Chopping up a human corpse is one thing. Drooling over it is quite another. I try not to think too much about it, but my growling stomach keeps pulling my focus back to axe and meat. A small part of me wonders if it's even necessary to cook the guy. Why not gather the small scraps of frozen thigh muscle that spatter the snow? Why not stuff them in my mouth and stop the hunger?

My stomach is a bitch. It's not even polite enough to send bile up my throat in disgust. Just a flood of saliva. *Feed me, feed me,* my body screams. There's no pretence left. I'm famished. *We* are famished, and the corpse is the only thing standing between life and death.

Despite the thick furs I'm wearing, warmth is sucked from my body at an alarming rate. A storm pummels my back, and fingers the gaps in my clothes. Throws splinters of ice against the narrow strips of my exposed skin. I pull my scarf higher and my hood lower, but three seconds later the wind has weaselled back in.

If the sea weren't covered with ice, it would be a roaring battlefield of grey and white, smashing against this black, flat rock that's Bear Island. It's mid-April now, and temperatures are still far below freezing. The ice holds. If I can't get our machine airborne again, we'll have to take our sled to the mainland. Both options are near impossible.

The only other alternative is to give up and die right here. I'm not ready for that.

It's four hundred kilometres and then some if we fly. More if we take the sled, because jumbled ice will force detours on us. Lots of them.

It's far. Too far for the tiny amount of food we have left. We can't wait this storm out. We can't hunt, can't leave, can't do a thing. Our food is running out. The man I'm cutting up is the last meat we have. Well...maybe not *quite*.

There are the three sled dogs we had to release because we couldn't feed them. They are running free on the island, catching seabirds. I saw them tear into an arctic fox once. Aside from us, the foxes must be the biggest animals here. I wonder when humans last visited this desolate place. And if they starved to death here.

I shake my head. No point thinking about that.

Before the storm rolled in, I took down two fat gulls. Blew their bodies to clouds of bloody feathers. I shouldn't even have tried, shouldn't have wasted ammo. My rifle is not for hunting small birds. It's made to kill people.

I should have hunted with bow and arrow, but that's Katvar's speciality. Problem is, he can barely see straight, let alone aim. And I suck at bow hunting. The even bigger problem is that the blizzard has dropped visibility to near zero, and all the birds have gone into hiding to wait out the storm.

Still, our dogs manage well enough. I've tried to steal what they catch, or at least find out where they're hunting. But they won't let me get close enough. They don't trust me anymore. I've cooked most of their pack members.

I've had no luck fishing, either. Wasted hours hacking holes into sea ice, hours waiting and freezing my ass off in this storm. For nothing.

There's only one source of calories left — the man I shot in Longyearbyen. Katvar and I have been skirting around the issue for the past two days. I don't know what it does to a person to eat another person. But we can't wait any longer.

I gaze down at the axe in my hand, at the chunk of hairy thigh I've severed. Fuck. We are about to eat one of the Sequencer's best sharpshooters, and I can't find a shred of regret in me. That's the biggest problem I have right now — I'm not even disgusted with myself.

I pull down my scarf and spit in the snow. Or mean to, but the wind smacks the saliva right back at me.

'How is your head?' I ask as I crawl into our snow hut and secure the entrance.

Katvar lifts a shoulder in a shrug. It's only been four days since a bullet grazed the side of his head. The memory of his limp body in the snow, a pink and scarlet cloud spreading around him, makes my throat tighten like a fist.

I swallow and hide the meat behind my back.

He lifts a hand to signal he's feeling better. I ask if he's hungry. Stupid question. Of course he is, but he pretends not to be.

He's set up the burner already. Snow is melting in a blackened pot. I drop the meat next to it, and tuck the bear pelt tighter around Katvar's frame. It annoys him, my hovering. He's still too pale, too haggard. We both are.

'Stew is coming up in a bit,' I say, trying a smile.

A jaw muscle feathers. He knows what's on the menu, but neither of us mentions it. I want us to live. Katvar's undemanding love has sneaked into the cracks of my black heart, and losing him would kill what little empathy I have left. The world could go to fucking hell if it weren't for him. I'm still breathing because of him. As unfathomable as it is, he loves me. Even my geography of scars, my chasm of darkness.

That's why I do what needs doing. For him, I stomp through the whiteout to a frozen corpse in the snow, axe in hand. And I'll keep doing it until we've eaten it all, and get out of this white hell. Until we make it, and dreams of food aren't mere fantasy. I'd kill for mashed potatoes with butter, string beans, and blood pudding. Or roast duck. The thought makes my legs buckle.

I crouch down and begin carving slices off the hunk of meat, drop them in the pot, and add a small handful of lichen for flavour. Or rather, to cover the flavour of human flesh. Whatever it tastes like. I haven't tried it yet.

I'd thought of cooking inside the airplane because I didn't want Katvar watching me do *this*. I don't want the scents clinging to our bedding long after we eat. I don't want to be reminded of this meal when I kiss Katvar's skin. But we can't afford to waste the heat from cooking with the little fuel we have left.

He's watching me. My neck prickles and my hands feel clumsy. I force myself to work fast. Shaving off the hair is the least I can do. I can't skin the thigh, because we need what little fat it provides. If I had butter, I would…

I swallow a mouthful of saliva.

'Did you know that before the Great Pandemic, people thought starving was sexy?' I say, and cut a sideways glance at him. He looks like he's waiting for the punch line. 'I'm not shitting you. They really thought this…' I wave at my bony frame, '…was hot. They starved themselves. Called it *dieting*.' Scoffing, I stir meat shavings into the pot.

Katvar cocks an eyebrow. 'No wonder they're all dead.' A noise draws his attention to the block of compacted snow that serves as the door to our hut. I hear it too. The dogs have caught the scents of our cooking. The wind carries their yapping. I crawl to the entrance and dig a gap in the snow. Ghostly shadows flit through the whiteout. Wind snatches barks from snouts, and hurls them out to sea.

Yep, I'm stalling. It's completely irrelevant whether the dogs are right here or farther away. The food isn't for them. It's ours.

The stew comes to a boil, and I switch off the burner and secure the lid, then wrap the pot in layers of reindeer skin. It takes longer to cook that way, but saves a lot of fuel. Tucking my chin against my knees, I shut my eyes and breathe slowly, conserving energy.

A rustling makes me look up. Katvar is moving on our bed of brush and furs. I ask how he's feeling.

He rolls his eyes. That's when I remember that I'd just asked him the same thing a few minutes before. His injury makes me nervous. It's not healing, and last night it started bleeding again.

'I want to take a look.'

'You just did this morning,' he signs.

'And I'll check it again and again until I'm happy with it.'

With a soft grunt, he lies back down, and lets me do my thing.

I undo the bandage around his head and check the sutures. Blood and clear liquid seep from torn skin. Looks exactly like it did a few hours ago. I spray disinfectant on the wound, just to make sure. Then I replace the bandages and gently press the gel pillow of the ultrasound scanner against the side of Katvar's head. I'm looking for dark spots. I'm terrified he might be haemorrhaging. But there's nothing.

He brushes his hand against my wrist and entwines his fingers with mine. 'Micka,' he croaks with his terribly damaged voice. 'Lie with me.'

Startled, I almost drop the scanner. He rarely ever speaks. His scarred vocal cords make speaking painful and taxing. A leftover from the infection that nearly killed him when he was a small boy.

'Rest for a bit,' he signs. 'Put your head on my shoulder.'

My vision swims. I swallow. 'Are you giving up?'

He shakes his head. 'I just want to hold my wife.'

His words tip me over the edge. The sharp precipice I've been walking for days. No — weeks, months.

A sob explodes from me, and I drop my head on his chest. He lifts a corner of our bear pelt and I sneak inside, curl a leg over his, wrap my arms tight around his frame that's painfully sharp from starvation.

It all pours out then. That I am terrified. That I don't want him to die. I can't remember ever *wanting* to live, but now I do. I want to live with him. I want to cross this stupid, unforgiving sea and find a nice, warm place for us. Eat lots and lots of food. Have kids together. Not worry about injuries, death, war, and the BSA every single moment of my waking hours, and every one of my nightmares.

Katvar draws soft circles on my temple with one hand, and on the small of my back with the other.

I wipe snot and tears from my face. 'So when the hell did we actually *marry*?'

He stiffens and draws back to look at me. 'I'm sorry. I shouldn't have——'

I grab his signing hands. 'Don't compare what *we* have, with what the BSA did to me.' *Did to me* makes those two forced marriages sound harmless. I was lucky with one, and not so...lucky with the other. Memories of my dead daughter rise, and I shove them back down.

Katvar's lids lower as his gaze slides to my mouth. He tugs me closer and kisses my temple.

'But, really,' I say. 'Did I sleep through the ceremony? The elders you picked must have sucked.'

Katvar snorts and I start to giggle.

'I don't need anyone to declare us husband and wife.' His signing is a bit awkward with me in his arms. 'I'm yours. As long as you want me. And...probably long after that.'

I shift to look at him. A severe mouth, dark eyes. 'I want you. But... But there's one thing I can't do. I can't have more than you.' That's my cringeworthy way of telling him that I'll never follow the tradition of his clan — the Lume — where women have several partners to increase the chance of survival for their children.

Understanding relaxes his features. 'I know. I would never ask that of you.'

I almost ask if his clan would demand it. But no, there's no going back for him. When he came of age, his clan banned him from ever choosing a wife because of what his father did to his mother. Katvar is the product of brother raping sister. To the Lume, he has "bad blood." That he and I are together violates one of their core values.

'What is it?' he signs.

'I'm sorry you can't go home because of me.'

His lips pull into a smile. He touches my face and curls his hand around the back of my neck. Pulls me in. Kisses me softly. And whispers against my mouth, '*You* are my home.'

Two

_____

Heartbeat.

The word tastes of honey at the back of my tongue. Like a sweet marble, polished and perfectly round. About to slip down my throat as I open my mouth to release its syllables. And as the last hard consonant dies away, the marble bursts open.

The flavour that bleeds from its core will depend on… many things.

When I lower my eye to the scope of my rifle and slide the crosshairs over the target, my heartbeat slows. When my index finger squeezes the trigger, and the round is fired, my heart pauses for a beat. And my mouth fills with flavours of tree bark.

Not just any tree. It's the constricting bittersweetness of

the ancient cypresses of Taiwan that creeps across my palate.

Then my heartbeat tastes of Basheer — Runner's name as a boy when the BSA killed his brothers and his father, all his clan, and dragged his sister and mother away. I wonder if he would mind if he knew that every time I stop someone else's heart, the taste of his childhood fills my mouth. I don't think he would. It was he who taught me killing.

Then there's the flavour I hope never to feel on my tongue again. It's the taste of a stutter. Of a compacted muscle that wants to give up, as I'm pressed to the floor by my second husband. A furry, scratchy, mouldy taste. I feel his heart beating against my back. His sweat.

My blood.

And then his.

I cut him open and bled him empty, the day after he murdered my newborn daughter.

I think of her every day. Of the day I was too weak to protect her. When grief digs its claws in too deep, I think of Katvar. His heart has a slow, deep rhythm. I want to wrap myself in it. Around him. Taste him. In a desert of ice and snow, the man with no voice has given me back my words and the flavours each of them carries. The BSA took them from me, and Katvar offered them back with a smile, a soft touch, and blueberries in reindeer milk.

Since then, his name tastes of exactly that: blueberries and reindeer milk.

He shifts and I open my eyes. The corners of his mouth curve. He reaches for me and trails his fingers through my hair. We could kiss, maybe even make love if we had the energy. We could forget our dire situation and make ourselves remember who we are. But I clench my teeth and say, 'Food is ready.'

THE STEW IS MOSTLY MEAT, water, and bits of green. The man was lean. I wish he'd been fatter. We need lots of fat to survive the Artic. We've been pushed beyond our physical limits. Have been for weeks. Our bodies are beginning to self-consume.

I unwrap the reindeer skin from the pot and divide the stew into two bowls. Katvar sits up without help. It's mostly stubbornness on his side. He doesn't want to look as weak as he feels. I don't tell him that I see right through him, as I hold out his bowl.

With trembling fingers, he accepts the food. And suddenly, I am deeply ashamed. I hated killing our dogs and cooking them for us. They were Katvar's friends and I took them away, one after the other. I told myself we would get over it. You do what you must to survive. You harden yourself. You get the fuck through it.

But at what point is the cost of survival too high? Can we eat this human and not lose our humanity?

Katvar and I hold each other's gaze as we lift the bowls to our mouths. It's like a silent agreement. *If you can do it, I can do it.* Each of us wants the other to survive.

He swallows. His eyes water as he clenches his teeth. Fuck, I know precisely what he feels right now. I stifle a moan. The meat is the opposite of what I expect. It's *delicious*. Tender, juicy, and quite similar to young mountain goat. Much, *much* better than dog.

'I checked for GPS trackers,' I blurt out for the sake of distraction. 'Found two and ripped them out. One in the cockpit, and a smaller one in the taillight. The battery is at nine per cent. We need a day of sun. And then…' I take a measured sip, so Katvar doesn't think I'm greedy. 'And then I just need to fix the broken ski. Maybe I'll salvage parts from the sled.'

His eyes flare. He sets the bowl down to sign, 'If you

cut the sled apart and can't fix the airplane, we are stuck here.'

'I know, but…' An idea starts creeping in. I take a big gulp of my soup and nod at Katvar's bowl.

He blanches. 'I don't think I can stomach another drop.'

I catch myself before asking if he doesn't like the taste. I could totally gobble up his leftovers. 'It's that or the dogs.'

He pauses, squeezes his eyes shut, and methodically forces the stew down his gullet. He's not going to eat another of his dogs, not if he can help it.

I follow his example and very nearly throw up. The knowledge of what we are eating and *enjoying* puts my stomach in knots.

'The aircraft is our biggest asset,' I say. 'We *have* to take it with us. The sled is less important. We can get a sled anywhere in the North, but not an airplane. We blew up the entire satellite network. Global communication is fucked, which means that getting from one place to another real fast will give us an edge.'

Katvar's gaze darkens.

I lower my bowl. 'I'm not in a warmongering mode. I'm just trying to not be stupid. The BSA are still around. We merely clipped their wings. But we clipped those of the Sequencers, too. Our main problem besides the obvious…' I tip my head at the empty pot, '…is that both organisations hate me right now. So once we cross to the mainland, we have to hide our machine. Keep it safe. If the Sequencers find it, so be it. But I'll blow it up before I let the Bull Shit Army get their dirty hands on it.'

'How do you hide a thing that big?' Katvar asks, but behind his eyes I see a strategy already blossoming. 'Is there a manual?'

'For the aircraft?'

He nods.

'Don't know. But we can see if it's in my SatPad.' I dig through my bag, thinking back to when Runner and I were crawling through the Taiwanese forest, our backpacks heavy with ammo and explosives, survival and communication gear. My hands still. I wonder if this war will ever be over. People have a tendency to keep pissing each other off on a global scale. So why try to end this war if some asshole is guaranteed to start another, two weeks later?

Katvar touches my shoulder and pokes his chin at my bag. 'What's this?' he signs.

I almost forgot I took this. 'It's an MIT FireScope.'

He lifts an eyebrow in question.

'I…um…found it in the Vault.'

He knows I'm not telling him everything, so he just waits.

I brace myself. 'I took it so we can sequence your genome.'

His throat works. He lifts one hand, then slowly the other to sign, 'Hope is a two-edged sword.'

'I know. But no hope at all is worse. Will you let me do it?'

He scans my face, and gives me a brief nod. I'm pretty sure I won't find any genetic defects, despite his being a product of inbreeding. I think of the large black tattoo on his chest: the Taker — the ritual knife the Lume fear and hate. The mere sight of the Taker and its obsidian blade hauls up in all the Lume a collective memory of infanticide. The knife is used to kill newborns who are too ill and weak to survive. Katvar said the Lume have little choice. For semi-nomadic hunters, a baby who will forever be sick is a danger to the health and well-being of all the others. They can't afford to raise a child who'll never be able to provide for the clan, who'll always need help to accomplish the smallest of tasks. To the Lume, the Taker is a bitter necessity.

And because Katvar is the child of brother and sister, the ritual knife was carved into his chest when he came of age, so that no woman would ever want him. So that there is not the slightest chance of him fathering defective kids.

But he's here, and I am not afraid. Chances are that our children, should we ever have any, will be healthy because he is healthy. But he himself needs proof. Something he can trust. To have a child who couldn't live would destroy him utterly.

I clear my throat. 'I used it only a couple of times. I have to read up on it again.'

'I'll do the reading. You have enough to do as it is.' He's been feeling useless and weak, but the curtain of insecurity is pushed away with one word. 'Priorities.' His hands cut through the air. He tugs the furs closer around his shoulders. 'I'll figure out what we need to get off the ground. Do you think the GPS still works?'

I shrug.

'And maybe it's not too late to tap into some kind of weather forecast?' He chews on his lower lip and frowns. 'The destruction of the global satellite network will be completed in a week, but if we're lucky a few weather satellites are still up there and can show us which way the storm is moving. Shit. We might be visible once the sky clears. But the Sequencers and the BSA will have bigger problems than to go looking for us. They are probably trying to get a fix on this.' He twirls a finger at the ceiling of our snow cave, indicating the burning satellites in the sky.

'Shit tends to hit the fan when I'm around.' I press my knuckles against my eyes until lights pop in my vision. 'Our main problem is food. We're running out of it, no matter what we decide to do next. We could take the sled, but we have only three dogs. None of them trust me, so they won't let me catch them. Even if they were already in their harnesses, it's four hundred kilometres to the mainland. We have three quarters of a corpse left. That's less than fifty kilograms of lean meat.'

'Brain has a high fat content,' Katvar interrupts.

'Ugh, thanks. Anyway. Flying shortens the travel time, but I don't know how to navigate the aircraft without a GPS. We have a compass and some old maps in the machine, but flying over sea ice, we'll have no reference points. We'll get lost.'

'How's that any different from when we found our way to Svalbard? You forget the Lume never had access to satellite navigation. Give me a stretch of clear sky and I'll tell you which way we're heading.'

'Oh, right. Okay, but…there's still the food problem.'

'Why not check if there's a book about Bear Island on your SatPad?'

I huff. Of course, I'd only ever checked how best to get *off* this island, not how to survive on it.

He grins at me. 'Show me how to work this thing.'

I log in, and tell Katvar that the SatPad uses voice recognition. I hold it to my mouth, say, 'I give operating rights to…' and shove it in his face.

He blinks, swallows, and croaks, 'Katvar.'

'Operating rights to Kark Var, please acknowledge,' the machine squeaks.

'Acknowledged,' I say, and give him an apologetic shrug.

He takes the SatPad from me and scoots back to give me more space. For a moment, I hesitate. I want him to rest, not work. But then, reading can be done in bed. Quickly, I show him the main functions of the SatPad, and then say, 'I'm going to check on the ice anchors. Make sure the storm can't move the machine. Or rip out the anchors and tear the aircraft to shreds.' My nerves are raw. I knuckle my thighs. So much can go wrong...*is* going wrong already.

He shifts his gaze to me, and brushes his fingers over my cheek. 'We are alive, Micka. We have food; we have ways to get out of here.'

We might have a little food left, but ways to get out of here? I can't see those, but I don't have the heart to tell him that. Not yet. I blink the burning from my eyes and look away.

'What?' he rasps. 'What's wrong?'

Shit. Most days Katvar sees straight into me. It's scary sometimes. Slowly, I pull in a breath and tell him. 'There was a rattling when I checked the ice anchors last night.'

He narrows his eyes. 'It was loud enough that you could hear it in the howling storm?'

I nod once and drop my head. 'I don't know how to get us out.' Admitting this to him is hard. I don't want him to lose what little hope we have left. My throat hurts. 'If there hadn't been a thick layer of snow covering the ice when I crash-landed, half the plane's belly would have been ripped open. The snow cushioned the landing, but I broke one of the skis and damaged the undercarriage. Something is loose, probably bent. Maybe even cracked. That's what's rattling. And the...' Angry, I slam a fist against my knee. 'The fucking storm has exposed the jumbled ice. We can't take off without a runway, and even if we had one, the landing gear would probably fall off before we got in the air. I screwed up. I'm... I'm so sorry.'

Three

Katvar grunts 'Uh-huh,' stares at the SatPad for a long moment, and signs, 'Once we reach the mainland, where are we heading?'

'Didn't you hear what I said?'

He lifts an eyebrow. 'Are *you* giving up?'

'I'm just being realistic.' Truth is, I'm exhausted. I haven't stopped running for months.

'Let's assume we make it, okay?' His expression is soft, as though I'm a wild animal that might bite if he's not careful.

I open my mouth to point out that we never thought we'd survive this trip, so naturally, I didn't plan *beyond* the impossible task of getting us to Norwegian territory, didn't fool myself into thinking anything more could be done. But somehow, Katvar's stoicism is infectious, and it lightens my exhaustion. 'Do the Lume have connections to the peoples of northern Scandinavia? Do you think we might find someone friendly with your clan?'

'I was with the Sami once, travelling with a small group of reindeer herders through Swedish territory. Birket would know if there are any tribes higher up north who are friendly with the Lume.'

Birket is chief of Katvar's clan. Or he was, when we left them. A wise man and a good leader. I liked his wry humour. 'I hope they are safe,' I say. The chances that the BSA haven't found the Lume, and retaliated for them helping me, are...slim.

Katvar doesn't look up as he nods. 'I need maps, a compass, paper and a pen, if we have any. The manual for the aircraft. Fifty kilograms of lean meat left, you said?'

'Less than that, I think.'

'In this cold, we're using up a lot of energy. I don't think lean meat alone is enough. We need a lot of fat, but meat is all we have, so...we'll probably need to eat about four kilograms each day.'

'Like, together?'

'No, each. That's eight kilos a day for the two of us. Which means...'

My stomach drops. 'Food runs out in four or five days.'

'Yeah,' he croaks, and runs his fingers over a stubbly chin.

'You are anaemic. You need to eat even more than that.'

He sits up straighter. 'Then I will eat more. Make stew. I'll do some thinking.'

WHILE KATVAR PLANS our next steps, I chop our corpse into five day's worth of rations. The brain will serve as our daily energy boost. I cut it into five parts, each about the size of a large duck egg. More than half of the brain tissue is fat. I hope I'll never again have to hack into a human skull, let alone turn its contents into dinner.

The liver will supply us with vitamins, and is divided into five portions as well. Then I put everything back in the airplane, out of reach of the dogs. I cut through the bones of the corpse's left arm, add today's ration of brain and liver to it, then push my way back through the storm and to our cave.

Katvar looks even paler now. He's shaking under the bear pelt. His lips are compressed, his speckled eyes, the colour of pine bark, are flat with fatigue. I take off my anorak and drop it on his shoulders, then start the burner and chuck meat, lichen, and snow into the pot. Funny, how quickly one gets used to eating human meat when extreme circumstances demand it. You survive, or you fucking don't.

I'd had worse. *Headquarters* — the word makes a mockery of that hell prisoners were put through. Memories of the scents of burning skin and hair, of blood and sweat and fear, still crawl up my nostrils at night. Screams, my own and those of others, echo down my throat. I had to make a small room in the back of my mind to stow away my monster and my nightmares. Every morning I shove them into that room, and every night they creep back out. Worst of all, I'm still undecided whether or not to put my dead daughter in that cell as well.

When I look up, I find Katvar's gaze resting on my face. He knows precisely what's going on. Knows that I don't want to be touched when I'm going *there*. Knows that, in moments like these, my monster hides just beneath my skin.

'Why is it that one always remembers the things one wants to forget?'

'Because pain is hard to ignore.' He clears his throat and asks, 'The battery's at nine per cent?'

Glad of the change of topic, I nod. The tiny bit of daylight that trickles through the whiteout has managed to charge the battery a fraction.

'To get off the ground, we'll need eight to ten per cent battery power.' Which pretty much sums up what I know about flying. There'd been no time to read the handbook, let alone take flying lessons before I stole my first solar plane. Same when I stole this one. But I guess when you kill the guys who own the thing, it's not really stealing. It's adopting, right?

'We can't wait for the sun to come out for a full charge. But maybe... Isn't there a way to use the wind for that?' he signs.

My heart bangs against my ribs. 'You are brilliant!'

He gives me a tired smile, and shakes his head. 'I don't know how to do it. Might just wreck the plane if I try.'

I scoot closer to him, alight with hope for once. 'I'm good with machines. Are there any diagrams? Did you see anything that looked like a wiring diagram in the handbook?'

He frowns. 'Not yet. I'll keep looking.'

'Maybe I can figure it out without a diagram.' I'll probably botch it, but there's no use in telling him that.

The water is boiling. I wait until the meat is thawed, then switch off the burner and wrap up the pot. Katar is scribbling away with pen and paper. I watch and wait for him to finish.

I serve our food and we eat in silence. He keeps looking at the numbers he's written, keeps flicking through the SatPad, and finally signs, 'Calculating takeoff distance under these circumstances is a bit of a gamble. The type of surface influences the distance we need. The rough snow and ice add to the distance, while low temperature lowers it. A tailwind would add distance, but we can't predict where the wind will come from or how strong it will be. Weight, configuration of the flaps, and how much power we use when taking off, all influence the takeoff distance. And the operating handbook is a mess.' He picks at the thing that is looking more like a bunch of rags with its heavy, bloated pages. The manual is going to fall apart as soon as the ice melts that holds its spine. 'I did find detailed climb performance, weight and balance information in *here*, though.' He taps the SatPad. 'I'm going to learn how to fly this thing properly.'

'But did you calculate it? The takeoff distance?'

'Three hundred to four hundred meters.'

'Oh…kay. I'll prep the runway, no problem.' We are so fucked. The storm has stripped the sea ice of its thick layer of snow. Now there's only jumbled ice around the aircraft.

'It will be more if we can't fix the nose ski.'

'I'll build a runway with compacted snow,' I say. It's more like an automatic response of my mouth than anything my brain would come up with. Because, really, do I look like I have four horses drawing a snow plow?

He gives me a tiny nod. Not convinced. 'This solar plane doesn't run on battery power. It's more like a…' His hands hesitate, then he just shoves the SatPad at me and taps the screen.

'*Ni-Co-Fe LDH?*' I read aloud. 'Oh, okay. Metal hydroxides, double-layered on nickel nano-foam by electrodeposition. It's a…' Surprised, I look up. Katvar has never so much as looked inside a motor. 'How did you know it's not a battery but a supercapacitor that generates hydrogen from solar power?'

He coughs and points to the last line on the screen. *Four high-efficiency dual-function stand-alone energy devices convert solar energy into electricity and hydrogen via a morphology-tunable nickel-cobalt-iron double hydroxide nano-foam in which hydrogen is also stored.*

'You were guessing?'

Katvar shrugs. 'I can tell you everything about sled dogs, but this stuff is bohemian villages to me.'

'What's bohemian villages?'

'That whole thing there. Had to read it ten times to understand that solar energy is converted and stored in those devices. I guessed that's what our batteries are.'

'I still don't get the "bohemian villages" thing.'

'Dog sledding used to be bohemian villages to you before I taught you about it. What you do with your rifle, how you can hit a reindeer that's a kilometre away is bohemian villages to me.'

'Oh, you mean that's all Greek to you?'

He snorts. 'No. Why would it be Greek to me? I *know* Greek.'

'You are fucking kidding me!'

He waggles his eyebrows and guffaws. 'You think we can build a runway? Won't that take…long?'

Wrong question. 'It will take longer if I just sit here and think about it.' I pull my furs back on, and move the compacted block of snow away from the entrance to our cave. As I tuck it back, taking care to leave no cracks for the wind to sneak in, I'm already making plans on how to build our runway, no matter how ridiculous the idea is. I'll use the broken ski as a shovel. Then I'll stomp the snow flat with my boots, so the wind can't blow it away. Maybe.

But I want to check the aircraft first, and tackle a problem that isn't as impossible as building a runway nearly half a kilometre long, maybe longer. With my bare hands. In the Arctic.

I push my way through the whiteout. Shards of ice are biting my cheeks just below my snow goggles. Maybe I should have eaten more. Light-headedness from under-nourishment stubbornly sticks to me.

Back in the airplane, I switch on all the controls to see if we can get a satellite image of the storm. But there's no connection. I wipe frost from the screens, and rest my chin on my mittens to think. Somehow we'll have to rewire the motor and generate wind power to charge the bohemian villages. The undercarriage needs fixing, and the dogs have to be caught. And I need to move and compress snow for a four hundred meter long runway. No problem if I had a few months. But there's not even a week's time. Five days is all we have. And this storm is so thick, the longer spring daylight hours aren't even helpful.

My brain sounds like an empty cave, echoing "We are fucked, we are fucked," with every breath I take. 'Shut up!' I growl, bite on my right mitten to pull it off so I can pull the manual from inside my anorak. I thumb through it, scanning for a section on the aircraft's landing gear.

There it is. I leave the book open on the cockpit floor and jump out to check the undercarriage. Big mistake, opening my mouth in the process. The wind freezes my teeth.

With my face up close to the landing gear, I push at the parts that should move. A faint clanking sound comes from the torque links that align the cylinder in the nose gear strut. I wiggle at it, which nearly freezes my fingertips to the metal, so I tap at it with my boot instead. And that's when the pin that connects the upper and lower torque links falls off and disappears into the snow.

Four

'Landing gear is fine,' I say when I shut the entrance to our hut.

Katvar's eyes briefly bounce up before settling back on the SatPad in his lap. 'This here says you didn't crash-land. As long as the machine is still airworthy, it was a hard landing, not a crash.' He is signing hastily without looking up from his reading. 'Not that it matters. With the landing gear fully functional, we'll just need to move the machine away from the jumbled ice out to the land-fast ice, and we can take off.'

'Okay.'

That's when he finally looks up. He cocks his head and narrows his eyes. 'What are you not saying?'

'Well, the…nose wheel is a bit… We can't steer with it.

But as long as we go straight ahead during takeoff, we're fine. No problem.'

'What about the ski?'

'It's a goner.'

A shudder racks his body. He draws the bear pelt tighter around his shoulders, and signs, 'I wish we had a tail dragger. The problem with tricycle aircraft is that the nose wheel is easily damaged on rough terrain and that's what happened here. We hit something during landing. Did you check if the nose wheel is restricted, or cocked at an angle?'

'Can't say whether it's restricted. I didn't try to move the machine. But it looks straight enough. The pin that holds the torque links came off, though. Can't fix the pin without a welding torch.'

'Hum,' he grunts, and scratches around the edges of his bandage. 'We have no ski for the nose wheel. We have no way of steering at low speed. We have no runway. We have no fuel beyond what's needed for takeoff. And our food runs out in a few days. If we… No. *When* we manage to take off and make it over the mainland, we'll have to find a runway, or risk flipping the machine when the nose wheel hits snow.'

'Okay. Which problem do we tackle first?' My voice is a bit squeaky. I clear my throat and try to look like that shit list of problems isn't giving me stomach cancer.

'Is it still light outside?' he asks.

'Yep. Another two hours.'

'Check the ice around the machine. See how far we have to drag it over the bumps. I'll cook, and find a place to land in Norway.'

'A HUNDRED KILOMETRES southwest of the Finnmark coast is a city,' Katvar signs when I return. 'It has an intact hydropower plant and its population is around seven thousand.'

I pull off my mittens and anorak, and rub my face with snow. 'That's big. How do they supply all these people with food and clean drinking water?'

'Norway got off pretty easy. They never had nuclear power plants, and from what I've heard from other clans, all of Norway, Sweden, and Finland remained neutral in the world wars. So the land's not contaminated by radioactivity. And they are too far north to be hit by cholera. But the weather changes were severe. When the Atlantic circulation ceased, all the temperate regions were plunged into subarctic conditions. And then came the hurricanes, devastating much of those territories until about three decades ago.'

I shed my fur boots and pants, and crawl into bed next to Katvar. 'If they had no disease or wars, shouldn't Scandinavia be full of people by now?'

He shrugs. 'Not enough hours of sunlight to grow grain and potatoes and such stuff. To live high up north, you have to hunt and herd reindeer, and migrate to the coast each summer to escape the mosquitoes. I've heard they can suck a grown man dry in twenty minutes.'

'Charming. And that's where we are heading,' I mutter. 'What about the people in that city you mentioned? How do they survive all that? What do they even eat?'

'I don't know.' He glances back at the SatPad. 'It doesn't say anything about it.'

Stretching my aching limbs, I yawn. The ceiling of our snow cave glitters in the light of an oil lamp. My fingers scrape a handful of snow from the walls to shove into my mouth.

Katvar moves from our bed to the pot he's wrapped in furs. He ladles stew into two bowls and hands me one. 'Have you found a way to get through the jumbled ice?'

When I stuff my mouth with a big piece of meat instead of answering, he averts his gaze and works his jaw. 'That bad?' his fingers ask.

'What isn't bad about *all* of this?' Anger makes me so hot, I kick the blanket aside. 'Don't worry, I'll figure it out.'

'Fuck, Micka. You still think you are alone? You still think no one can help you?' He thumps his chest. 'I am right here.'

'But you are injured.'

'I'll be dead if we can't build this runway. I'm well enough to shovel some snow.'

I fill my mouth with more stew. I don't want to point out that just taking a leak behind the hut is a huge effort for his damaged body. And so I eat, silently hoping he'll drop the issue.

'How far?'

Of course, he doesn't drop the issue. I shut my eyes and swallow. 'If we go in a straight line, it's three hundred meters to smooth sea ice. If we go in a crooked line, it's about four hundred meters, but easier to manoeuvre through. The absolute minimum time needed to move snow and press it down hard is one hour per meter, three meters wide. That's three hundred to four hundred hours to build our runway. Two weeks if we work without sleeping and eating.'

My teeth hurt from all the jaw clenching.

He touches his fingers to my cheek. Breath rasping through his windpipe, he says, 'We are alive.'

Yes. But for how long?

As if he's heard my thoughts, he smiles faintly and signs, 'You don't need to be superhuman. All you need is

29

courage, enough to get yourself through the day. One day at a time, Micka. One day at a time is enough.'

I WAKE to the guttering light of our small oil lamp. Too tired to check the level of fuel left in it, I turn my face into Katvar's back. Faint trembling runs up and down his spine. 'You okay?' I whisper. 'Katvar?'

He groans.

Icy dread crawls over my skin. 'Katvar!'

He curls to a ball and shifts a palm over his ear. 'Too loud.'

'I'm sorry, I'm sorry,' I whisper. 'Do you have a headache? I'll get the ultrasound scanner.'

My fingers fumble with the small machine, nearly dropping the gel pillow as I move it to his head. I need him to be safe. I can weather all that life throws at me as long as he's alive and well. My heart thunders against my ribcage, and doesn't even calm when the ultrasound scanner shows no dark regions where the bullet grazed his head. He's the shelter of my heart. I can't go on, won't go on, if he dies.

He shudders again and asks for a sip of water. I pass him a handful of snow and prep the burner to make tea. Or what passes for tea now — hot water with a few crumbs of pathetic lichens.

'Your gums…' *Are bleeding.* I don't finish the sentence. Scurvy. Another thing we don't need.

Holding the melting snow in his mouth, his features relax. He grabs another handful and gingerly brings it to his forehead. A sigh, and his eyes find mine. 'Just a headache. And a bad dream. Sorry I woke you.' His signs are slow and clumsy.

'Promise to wake me up if you don't feel well. Okay?'

A smile. But it doesn't reach his eyes. Once the water is hot and he has drunk his fill, he signs, 'I thought about the runway.'

I bite my tongue to hold in a nervous laugh. He's been thinking about the runway, as ill as he is.

'Take off the two intact skis. Rip everything out of the plane you don't need. Then get the dogs to pull the machine over the jumbled ice. The dogs and you can make it. Together. And then...' He drops his arms, exhaustion making his breath fragile.

I do the math: On our way from the Carpathian Mountains to Svalbard, the maximum weight the dogs had to pull was five hundred kilograms per sled. With a dozen dogs for each sled, each animal pulled about forty kilograms for several hours each day. Now we have only three dogs and over a tonne of weight to pull. So I *only* have to reduce the weight of the machine by...what...eight hundred kilograms? No, it *will* work. It *has* to. The dogs will only have to pull the machine for three or four hundred meters. If I help with a lever to move the wheels over the bigger ice chunks...

'I'll do it. And I'll rewire the motor. We'll make it. Just promise me to take it easy, okay?'

'And when you are ready to leave, put a ski on the nose wheel. Forget the other two wheels. The nose wheel...' His arms tremble. 'Nose wheel is important. You need...a ski on it.' He drops his hands and clenches his teeth. 'Need... sleep,' he croaks.

I watch his lids lower, shocked that he's planned my escape without ever mentioning his own.

When you *are ready to leave.*

I'll never be ready to leave him.

Five

The manual is a piece of shit on a stick, especially the sections covering the engines. The diagram shows eight-cylinder engines, but my engines actually have only six. I don't know who's put in the air filters, but they look like they were made when the dinosaurs were still around. Or maybe made by dinosaurs.

On the plus side: The storm has lessened, allowing me to open the hatches without having to shovel snow off the engines every two minutes, and the starter motors are where they're supposed to be. Those are the things I need to rewire, so they don't pull electricity to turn the propellers, but instead use wind energy to produce electricity and feed it through the charge controllers and into the bohemian villages — aka supercapacitors. Any dumbass could do this because it's really just cutting the two connections that run from each starter motor to its battery, and plugging them into the charge controller instead.

Well…as long as one doesn't mix up the salad of wires and relays. So maybe not a project for dumbasses after all.

Right now, my main problem is that the wires I just cut off are too damn short. I need them to be about a meter and a half longer to connect to the charge controllers. So I shut the engine hatch, climb into the aircraft, and scan for something to scrounge. The light fittings seem like a good choice. I search the interior for a toolkit and come up empty. Who flies this thing without a toolbox on board?

My knife should do. I use the blunt edge as a screwdriver and the sharp edge as a…well, *knife*. The wall panels go; they are basically just decoration. I gut the interior, rid it of padding and screens — because the aircraft needs to lose weight anyway — and find what I need: wires feeding into outdated LEDs. The copper wires are thin; there's a risk they'll vaporise. I rip them out anyway, and get back to rewiring the first starter motor.

After engaging the starter motor with the engine shaft, I step back and give the propeller a good shove. One lazy flop, and it stops. I try again. Same result. Shit. If I can't move the props, how can the wind move them? Trying harder, I hear a dull *ungh-ungh*. I slap my forehead. The drive shaft is still engaged to the combustion engine, which means…

My heart drops to my toes. Is it even possible to disengage it?

I scramble back to the cockpit and thumb through the manual. There's no mention of disengaging the drive shaft from the engine, but I find a diagram. It makes me feel sick.

Each propeller is permanently linked to its drive shaft, which is permanently linked to its combustion engine.

In short: I can't use the propeller to generate electricity and hydrogen.

Groaning, I smack the stupid manual against the wall.

Okay. Deep breath. This isn't the end. If I can make our aircraft lighter, it can climb higher, and once it's above the clouds, the sun can charge the bohemian villages and refuel the machine.

Numb from cold and faked courage, I reconnect the starter motor and shut the engine hatch, then continue ripping everything out of the interior we don't need. But it's all light stuff so far. The real culprits are screwed to the floor panels: four passenger seats. And no wrench on board. And…oh, shit. They didn't use hex bolts — those would have been somewhat easy to remove with a makeshift wrench. Nope, some dork — and I'm guessing it was the same who decided a toolkit was unnecessary baggage — used socket screws.

For a brief moment, my trigger finger tingles, itching to fire a bullet into each bolt and be done with it. I consider my axe, but doubt it would do anything but put a few nicks into the aluminum legs of the seats. Although I *really do* feel like putting my axe to this fucking thing.

'Right,' I mutter, and stomp back to our snow hut and our half-buried sled in a snow drift. Saw in hand, I return to the aircraft and cut a slot into each bolt. They are made of steel so it takes ages, and leaves the saw pretty much useless for anything but cutting blocks of snow for an igloo. With the final bolt loosened, the seats go flying out the door, and I'm so exhausted I'm ready to pass out. Drenched in sweat, I drag myself back to our snow hut.

Just to find Katvar gone.

I hurry back out to search for him. Snow is still falling,

near horizontally, but visibility has improved. Shadows move ahead of me. Huffs and excited barks. And then I spot Katvar among our three fur balls, squatting in the snow, receiving nose kisses and bumps to his chest.

'You all right?' I ask. The dogs eye me warily, but with Katvar close by, they seem to feel safe.

He looks up at me and smiles. For the first time in days, he seems to be improving. I'm so relieved my vision blurs.

He pulls off his mittens and signs, 'Just wanted to check on the dogs.'

'You feel better.'

'I do. But I messed up our lunch. Dropped in all the salt we had left. Sorry. Do you want me to strap the dogs back into their harnesses?'

WE LEAVE the dogs unrestrained for now, because we can't feed them. Katvar will try to catch them in a day or two, whenever the aircraft is ready to be moved. I tell him that I've managed to peel off the skis that were frozen to the back wheels without breaking them. And I tell him that we can't power the bohemian villages with wind.

He lights the burner, places the pot on our small stove, and stirs stew without acknowledging the new information. 'It's all yours,' he signs a few minutes later.

'But you have to eat!'

'I already ate.'

'Oh? Your appetite is back? That's great.' I spoon the food into my mouth and don't even waste a single thought on who it is I'm eating. Partly because of all that salt scorching a hole into my tongue.

Katvar slips his boots off, sheds fur pants and anorak, and sits on the bed with the bear pelt around his bony frame. Eyes stuck to his socked feet, he signs, 'I thought... I thought I'd die. I couldn't see straight, the headache was... the worst I ever had. I didn't even know what I put into that stew until I got real thirsty from it. All our salt, gone. I'm sorry.' A strand of dark brown hair slips over the bandage around his head and dips against his cheek.

I brush it away softly, and rest my palm on the side of his face. 'I don't care as long as you're feeling better.'

'It was strange. Suddenly the headache was gone. As if a weight was lifted.'

'You really needed to eat.'

He nods, takes my hand and kisses my wrist. 'I don't want to be useless. I don't want to let you down. But I am, and I do.'

I shed my furs and crawl into bed with him. 'I suck at pep talk, but... I couldn't do any of this without you.' I wrap an arm around him and kiss the divot between his collar bones. 'I wouldn't even try.'

He stares at me long and hard.

I touch my fingertips to his lips. 'You've *never* been useless and you've *never* let me down, and I doubt you ever will.'

His gaze rests on my mouth, then travels up to my eyes. That's when I notice that one of his pupils is much larger than the other. It must be a symptom of concussion.

He lifts a hand and signs letter by letter, 'Promise me to go on if I can't.'

That punches all air from my body. 'No.'

Groaning, he leans his head against mine. 'I can't imagine a world without you in it.'

'But I am supposed to?'

He chuffs. 'I guess we'll both have to cling to life like the devil, then.'

'Speaking of which. We'll leave everything behind we

don't absolutely need. I'll see if I can find some more stuff to rip out of our aircraft. Do you think you can calculate how much lighter we have to be to get above the clouds?'

'We need to know how high the clouds are.'

'Yeah. Shit. I have no idea.'

'I'll make an educated guess,' he signs and trails his fingertips through my short hair.

'I want to give you something.' I've been thinking about this since we got here, but he's never been well enough.

I pull a leather string with a silver rectangle attached to it from around my neck. It glints in the lamplight. The small dog he made for me is nestled right next to it. I undo the knot and slip the silvery piece off the string, then pull a new leather string from my pocket. 'When I was a prisoner, this was the only thing that kept me alive in my darkest time. This was my purpose. Without it, I would have ended myself. And now…I don't need it anymore. I mean, I don't need it to remind me to live. But…this small thing means so much to me. It brought me to *you*. It's the exabyte drive with all the software and access codes I used to destroy the satellite network.'

Katvar's lips compress. He produces a stiff nod, and his Adam's apple bobs.

'Do you not…want it?'

He grabs my hand and presses a kiss to my palm. Without taking his eyes off me, he lowers his head so I can tie the exabyte drive around his neck.

Six

Softly rolling hills stretch from horizon to horizon. Upon the scorched earth lie scorched bodies. Here and there, a hand scratches at the grey sky — a final attempt to claw itself out of hell. Smoke curls up from ribcages, gaping jaws, and empty eye sockets. The air is thick with the stink of burnt meat.

'Micka!'

My name crackles across my eardrums, rough as weathered asphalt, spreading flavours of pear and ash across my tongue. Gradually I grow aware of my body, as though only moments earlier I'd been a mere idea. I gaze down at myself. In my right hand, I find a torch.

I scream.

A hand in my hair.

A soft caress.

As the dream fades, I reach out and pull Katvar closer,

press myself against his warmth. His scents of sweat, pine needles, dog fur, and dry bracken steady me. My mouth finds his, and he yields to me, to my tongue, my hands, my desperation.

THE GASTROINTESTINAL TRACT of a human is six to seven meters long. I actually looked that up, just in case my twine isn't long enough. It's not. But six or seven meters won't help much anyway. And then there'd be the mess…

But let's not dwell on it.

My twine collection is nearly fifty meters long. Three hundred would be better, but it seems like the Bear Island shopping mall just ran out of twine. When I was Erik's prisoner, I once read about shopping malls in one of his books. Couldn't wrap my head around the concept, and still can't: aisles upon aisles of food; whole buildings ten times bigger than any council house I've ever seen, stuffed to the roof with food. Is that why they believed starving was sexy, because they had no idea what starvation meant? Were people back then happier than people today?

I think of the Nenets who laughed so much, their faces crinkled like old leather all around the eyes. They *did* have a lot of food, though.

I would definitely be much *much* happier if Katvar and I had enough food.

My stomach yowls. I drop the axe and look back at the three narrow paths I've managed to chop into the jumbled ice, back along the twine I tighten between the nose wheel and one of the passenger seats I dragged out to mark the direction I need to go. There's a second, shorter length of twine with three pieces of cloth tied to it to mark the distance between the three wheels of the aircraft. The disheartening part is that I've only managed to get about fifty meters through the jumbled ice so far. Two hundred and fifty meters left to go. I'm too slow, despite me kicking my own ass all the time, and I've only been taking out the biggest chunks of ice.

I guess I should eat a bite before I get back to work.

KATVAR SITS IN BED, frowning. His whole body frowns as his hand furiously scribbles at the notepad. He doesn't look up when I enter the snow hut, just flicks through the SatPad and gets back to writing. I set up the burner and make food, take off my furs and rub my face with snow. I leave his portion in the pot as I silently eat mine. And then I leave.

THREE HOURS LATER, and I'm halfway through the jumbled ice. They look like shit, these gouges I've made.

Back in the hut, I grab the pot — which is now empty and washed — and fill it with snow. Parched, I begin to make tea, when Katvar drops his pen and notepad, and stares up at the ceiling.

I want to say a lot of things to him, but don't: *How's your head? Food runs out tomorrow. Have you found a way to make the aircraft lighter?*

The water in the pot begins to simmer, so I switch off the burner, and add a few crumbs of lichens. 'Talk to me, Katvar.'

'I don't trust this. I don't trust myself. I was already wrong about the takeoff distance. So how can I know if *this* is correct?'

I pour tea into our bowls, and hand him his. 'Walk me through.'

He explains the difference between ground roll and takeoff distance, the weight of the bohemian villages at full capacity versus the weight they have now. He explains how much weight we have to lose to get the machine above the clouds, which might or might not be at two thousand five hundred meters altitude.

'Okay, so you are saying the ground roll is much shorter than the takeoff distance. But that doesn't matter to us. We have to get the machine out of the jumbled ice first, and beyond that are a couple of hundred kilometres of smooth sea ice. About the weight, though...'

'Yeah,' he rasps.

We need to lose two hundred kilograms to get to an altitude of two thousand five hundred meters with the few dregs of fuel we have left. 'Okay,' I say, and put my furs back on. I'll chop the shit out of the jumbled ice, gut that stupid aircraft and get us out of here.

'Micka,' Katvar croaks before I can leave.

'I've found something.' His hands are trembling as he signs.

More bad news. I lock my knees so they don't buckle.

'I was searching for more information on the SatPad, and I found a submenu, and then another one, a hidden one. And there was...was...' He lowers his head, swift fingers flying over the SatPad's screen. He holds it out to me, eyes black as tar.

I sit down and stare. 'W...what? Two million... *Two million books?*'

Katvar nods.

'Why would Erik leave this behind? Are you sure they are books?'

'I opened forty or fifty at random.'

'All about religion and warfare?'

'No, they are...stories. Crime stories. Love stories.

41

Handbooks on how to build things, make things. Medical books. It's…a miracle.'

'*Two million books?*'

He nods again.

'Fuck me in suspenders! But why?'

'A backup, maybe?'

I lean back and nearly fall over. 'Maybe. I have to think about this.'

'We can make copies and distribute them everywhere. People need this.' He taps his knuckles against the SatPad, his breath ragged.

'It's most likely a trap. Erik doesn't leave things like this laying around. Impossible. It's… Could it be rigged?' I snatch the SatPad, and scoot close to the exit. Scan the seals and tiny screws. Lots of scratches there.

'If it hasn't blown us up yet, it's not going to blow us up now. Or tomorrow.'

'I don't trust this.'

He puts a hand on my knee. 'I don't either. But it's an asset. He hid it in the Vault. It wasn't just laying around. It was *hidden*, Micka.'

'But he knew I was coming.'

'Yes, and he had *you* rigged. He tried to blow *you* up. He didn't want to blow up his library.'

'What…did you…' My mind begins to race. When Katvar lifts his hands to speak, I grab his wrist and shake my head. I need a minute. 'Erik said something when he gave me this thing. Ugh, I'm so stupid! He wanted me to figure it out! He said, "I'm giving you access to part of my library." *This* is his library and he gave it to me. He gave me access to *part* of it, and even said it. But I never expected the SatPad to contain *all* his books.'

I release Katvar's hand and shake my head. 'Erik kept harping on about "knowledge is power." He gave me two million books, knowing I could read whatever I wanted. Learn whatever I wanted. But only if I was smart enough to find them. And I never was.'

Groaning, I rub my tired eyes. The Great Pandemics and the World Wars have left humanity bereft of written knowledge. Burning books, blowing up servers, murdering doctors, scientists, political leaders was all part of eradicating cultures and expertise. Part of weakening your enemy. But what I am holding in my hand now is…unfathomable. It's the most valuable thing we have in our possession. More valuable than a hundred solar planes. 'What do we do with it?' I whisper.

'We can change everything. We can change the world.'

———

THE WIND HAS PICKED up again. It's an angry storm of shards. Instead of chopping away at the ice, I work in the aircraft, a list from Katvar flattened out on the cockpit controls. I cross off the four passenger seats, six kilos each. We're down by twenty-four kilos. One hundred seventy-six to go. The floor mats and interior panels weigh approximately four kilograms together and I've tossed them out already, so I cross those off, too. All the access panels in the floor make only about two kilos in total. I leave them in for now.

Below the list of items in the airplane's interior is our packing list. Axe, saw, bow and arrows, guns and ammo, furs, brush for our bedding, dogs, harnesses and lines, sled, burner, pot, bowls. The armfuls of brush are light, but we'll leave them behind because they aren't essential. The sled weighs about fifty kilos. The pot and bowls another two. A no-brainer really. I cross them off the list.

One hundred twenty kilos left to kill.

The dogs weigh about thirty kilos each. Three dogs. I cross them off.

Thirty kilos left.

My rifle weights eleven kilos, the ammo about three. Shit. Shit shit shit!

If I can't defend ourselves, there's no point of flying to the mainland.

I sit down in the pilot seat. My hands travel along the armrests. My gaze follows. How heavy are these things? They aren't on Katvar's list, but I wager they are about ten kilos each.

It takes a while to cut a slot into each screw of the co-pilot seat, and unscrew it with my knife. The thing feels heavier than the passenger seats, which is good. It lands with a dull *whomp* in the snow.

Twenty kilos left, and the innards of the aircraft are already naked. There's not a speck I can toss out. Jamming my hands into my fur sleeves, I scan the interior again.

The radio, maybe? No, it won't be much heavier than half a kilogram and we'll need a way to communicate. But if we don't get off this island, we won't need to communicate with anyone.

Ever.

If I had a wiring diagram, I could rip out anything that needs satellite connection, but…I don't.

My gaze falls on the pilot seat. Ten kilograms of luxury butt warmer.

Fuck it.

I drop to my knees, pick up the saw and get to work.

Seven

The storm has calmed to a sluggish breeze, but the sky is still covered in thick clouds that vomit snowflakes the size of quail eggs. I've been chopping ice for only a few minutes, but I'm already sweltering in my thick furs. Hoping I haven't caught a cold, I pull off my anorak and toss it on a large block of ice. My boot hits slush. Baffled, I lift my leg to find a puddle. Staring at the tiny pond at my feet, I touch my forehead. Nope. Definitely no fever.

It must be…spring?

The axe drops from my hands. I race out through the jumbled ice toward the land-fast ice beyond Bear Island. I rip off my snow goggles and pull down my scarf and collar. Between the cold snowflakes kissing my face, the air feels…balmy?

It's not me feeling off, it's the weather. I reach the land-fast ice to find a doughy covering of snow. I touch my fingertips to it. The biting cold is gone. The crisp sharpness of the snow has turned sodden. Sticking a handful of it into my parched mouth, I turn back to scan the island. The jumbled ice belting the shoreline is more than a meter and a half thick — or was — when I carved my fishing hole. A few days of warm weather won't melt the ice cover, but... How much pressure will the melting ice tolerate before tidal forces break it free?

As I wash my face with wet snow, it hits me: If I'm fast enough, the weather might help me move the solar plane. Only three shallow trenches of sixty meters each left to cut. If they fill up with a few centimetres of meltwater, the dropping night temps will freeze the paths smoother. The dogs and I won't have to work so hard to pull our machine across to the flat land-fast ice. But...shit. The wheels will freeze to the ground.

Okay. One problem at a time.

I walk back, pick up my axe and anorak, and make my way to the hut.

KATVAR DIGS through our SatPad and our aircraft's manual for information on ground roll under these changing conditions. He comes up empty. On tarmac runways, ice, slush, and water double the ground roll. Maybe even triple it. But a runway that's made of ice and covered with puddles of meltwater and mushy snow? Total unknown. Our main problem, though, isn't the increase in ground roll, it's that we'll need two or three times more fuel to get the machine off the ground.

Fuel we don't have.

'The solution is simple,' Katvar signs, after a lot of nodding to himself. His right pupil is still larger than the left, and it doesn't seem to react to light. That worries me. But what worries me more is that he has this glassy stare and stiff set to his jaw that tell me his headache is back.

What he signs next pulls up my hackles: 'Leave everything behind. Every piece of equipment except your knife, rifle, and ammo. That will make the machine light enough to get above the clouds with the little fuel that's left. Refuel above the clouds, fly to the mainland, hunt, keep refuelling, and come back to get me. We'll eat and rest, and then fly back out together.'

'You want to…stay here, so the plane is lighter?' I have to make sure my ears aren't playing tricks on me.

One nod.

'I'm not leaving you behind.' I *so* won't budge on this.

He wraps his fingers around my wrist, and signs with his free hand, 'Please, love.'

'Forget it.'

He freezes. Sets his chin. 'It's the only solution, and you know it. Micka, *please*.'

'You can force me to tie you up and drag you into the solar plane, but you cannot make me discard you like a rabid dog.' I leave my furs in the hut. There's ice I need to attack.

Katvar's eyes shiver beneath his pale lids. I wonder if he's dreaming of food. I dream of food all the time. And of war. Rape. Burning bodies. Sometimes even when I'm wide awake.

But graver problems demand my attention now. There's nothing left to eat. We've boiled the last bones, sucked out the last shred of marrow, licked the final drops of broth from the bottom of our pot.

We're out of time.

As I wait for the sunrise and watch Katvar sleep, I let my decision soak into my bones. And strangely, it calms me. There's no good solution to this mess we're in, and the few options we have left for saving ourselves are all suicidal. Such as taking off with only a handful of fuel.

When I shut my eyes, I can see us crashing on the ice. A quick death. Better than a slow perishing, withering to a pair of frozen skeletons.

Leaving him here and returning in two days is the lowest-risk option, but only for myself, and only if I don't break off the nose wheel when I land, or run into problems on the way.

There are no guarantees.

I don't understand why Katvar thinks so little of himself. As if he's mere ballast. Does he not know that I am nothing without him? That there's no reason for me to save myself, if I can't take him with me?

His heart has not been sullied by the brutalities the BSA dishes out. He is the opposite of Runner who was a sniper and strategist with a healthy kill rate under his belt, a man with a darkness so deep and tightly coiled up inside him that kissing him felt like unleashing a hurricane. Katvar has none of that, and yet much more. He's my bright light in all this darkness that I am. He is the bearer of my humanity. Without him, I will burn down the world.

In his gentle hands, Katvar cradles my soul.

THE ANXIOUS WHINES of our three sled dogs trickle through the thick walls of our snow hut. The quiet hours before sunrise are probably the best time to hunt; the dogs are anxious to leave. Or perhaps they're just bored of being tethered to a block of ice the whole night. Just a little longer, buddies.

My gaze scans the two piles of items: the things I'll take with me — Katvar, the furs to wrap him up, my knife and my pistol plus an additional clip, our pot and burner, my skis. And what I'll leave behind — the ultrasound scanner, MIT Firescope, SatPad, and defibrillator we stole from the Vault, my rifle and ammo. All has been wrapped up tightly in reindeer skins. Katvar's bow and arrows, our oil lamp, three dogs, stay behind as well. And much more. It's hard to leave my rifle here, but I can defend us with the pistol if it comes to it. I'll search for elk or reindeer before I land the machine, then strap on my skis and intercept them, kill one or two with my pistol. We'll eat, rest, and refuel, then fly back to get our stuff and the dogs.

THERE'S STILL a little time before sunrise. I should try to catch some sleep, but somehow I'm unable to let my control slip. I check my pile of things again when my eyes fall on one of our packages. Following a whim and with nothing else to do, I untie the twine holding the reindeer skins together, and dig for our SatPad to search for "Bringer of Good Tidings." The first time I heard this tale, I couldn't believe my ears.

The Bringer of Good Tidings sent a woman with hair the colour of flames and skin as scarred as a battlefield to free humanity. She is the spark. The people are the force.

Birket, chief of the Lume, told me that tale when he helped me escape an overzealous Sequencer who believed I'd aided the BSA and murdered my own friends. The tale was spread among hunter tribes of Eurasia, even as far up north as the remote Nenets territory. Birket believed it is I who will *free humanity*. Whatever *that* means.

I grip the SatPad harder when my search returns a single hit. Ribbons of goosebumps pour down my back.

The Bringer of Good Tidings is mentioned several times in the Qur'an. I think I'm going to retch. Religious crap! What else would the Bringer of Good Tidings be, if not some religious propaganda?

Fuck, I really should have connected the dots earlier. When I was a prisoner of the BSA, Erik shoved his so-called *holy* books down my throat, expecting me to learn them by heart. But I was terrified of what he might do next, what punishment and torture I might have to endure if I couldn't rattle down text that never made any sense to me, too terrified to learn, to think. Busy with escape plans and my own fears, I never tried to understand what he was trying to teach me.

Looks like I was right all along. I'd been suspicious of Erik from the first time I heard this "good tidings" tale. But… Something never fit. Something was always off.

And still is.

The Bringer of Good Tidings sent a woman with hair the colour of flame and skin as scarred as a battlefield to free humanity.

Why would Erik spread this among hunter tribes? And how? What *would* the BSA be hoping to accomplish by motivating people to idolise me?

Ah, right. Erik was planning to use me as a girl mascot. Put me up in some pseudo-leader position to draw more women to the BSA, because the *Brothers and Sisters of the Apocalypse* need fresh meat. They're all rapists, and everyone knows it. As if people would be stupid enough to believe propaganda and ignore their own experience.

Maybe they *are* stupid enough.

But *free humanity?* If there's one thing humanity needs to be freed of, it's the BSA.

No, I can't see Erik spreading this tale. I'm missing

something here. I have the feeling it's staring me smack in the face, and I'm too blind to catch it.

I skim chunks of text about the Bringer of Good Tidings and learn that he's the Prophet Muhammad, sent by Allah to give glad tidings and warn all mankind. But of what? I find a lot of "if you don't worship Him, you'll be punished" crap. There's nothing new here. I could cut these sections out and paste them into the Bible, and no one would notice the difference.

There's even a list of other names used for Muhammad. I snort. He was called "The Model of Conduct" and "The Perfect Man." Yeah. Sure. Women are *never* that. In these shit pamphlets, women are never persons to look up to, but chattel a man can steal, trade, rape or beat to a pulp.

This is what the BSA is using: fiction books that are more than two millennia old. I wouldn't be surprised if Erik started to call himself "Prophet" sometime soon. I freeze when I find Muhammad's other names: the Bearer of Good Tidings, the Announcer — *al-Mubashir, al-Bashir.*

Al-Bashir.

I swallow.

My knuckles come down on my mouth with too much force. The taste of blood spreads on my tongue as I whisper Runner's childhood name, 'Basheer.'

My brain stutters, unable to process the new information because it's just too unbelievable…yet…shockingly logical.

My eyes squeeze shut when I think of Runner whispering poetry across my skin: *I grew up in the desert. I love it. It's such a beautiful place. I love the sand, the wild landscape scarred by countless battles, the sunsets.*

The scarred landscape was my skin. The sunset, my hair. If Runner had wanted to let me — and only me —

know who's spreading this tale, he'd use the name he told no one else. The name he'd been given by his mother. A name he'd kept until the day the BSA killed his tribe and his family.

Basheer, the Bringer of Good Tidings.

There was never a reason for Erik to spread propaganda that would motivate people to help me. Runner, though, had *every* reason.

Skin as scarred as a battlefield. Runner's words on the day I left him to die.

And suddenly, the whole thing makes sense.

The Bringer of Good Tidings sent a woman with hair the colour of flames and skin as scarred as a battlefield to free humanity. She is the spark. The people are the force.

Runner gave his life and this final gift to me. He stayed in Taiwan to radio this tale out into the world. To help me survive and raise a shitstorm. All for the tiny chance the tale would spread and I'd be able to make my escape. He was a strategist, an expert in the art of war. Posturing often decides a battle before it even begins. And propaganda plays a big part in it.

I don't need to shut my eyes to see him hunched over the mic, repeating the tale over and over and over again. Hoping I would make it.

I cannot fathom what made him so sure I'd survive the BSA when no one else ever had. Did Runner even ask the Sequencers to evacuate him? He must have. He couldn't have chosen that ugly radiation death just to…

He *couldn't* have…

Choking, I press my face into the crook of my arm.

Eight

Katvar is still in bed when the heavy sky faintly blushes. He's tossing and turning, but asleep. I move our few things to the airplane, free the wheels and nose ski of ice, then return to our hut. The dogs draw back when they see me stomping through the snow.

I push open the entrance and kneel at Katvar's side. It worries me that he's still not up. 'Hey,' I say softly, and touch his cheek.

He cracks open his eyes, scrunches up his face, and rolls over to retch in the snow.

Ice hits my stomach. 'Is…is your head hurting?'

He grunts and claws at his temples. That's a yes.

I unwrap the bandage. He tries to hold still, but pain and nausea send shivers through his body. His arm is oddly stiff. I try not to dwell too much on what that could mean.

I scrape a few handfuls of snow from the walls of our hut and hold them to his wound. With a hoarse cry, he lashes out, pushing me away — an awkward and jerky movement that seems disconnected from his body.

'Sorry,' he croaks. 'Didn't…' Gnashing his teeth, he rolls off the bed and presses his face to the ground. Snow muffles his groans of pain.

My mind disconnects itself from my frantic heart, and calculates options and outcomes. My calm hands untie our travel package, find the MedKit, and pull out a syringe and a small bottle of painkiller. I pull down Katvar's collar to expose the muscles of his neck and shoulder, swipe disinfectant over his skin, and inject ten milligrams of morphine. I don't know if morphine can be given intramuscularly, but the label on the bottle lists a maximum dose. So that's what he's getting. For now.

With my hand on the back of his neck, I wait and watch. Gradually, his breath becomes less laboured.

'Does it help?' I whisper.

He nods once.

'Good. We're leaving now.' Before he can protest, I flip him around, grab him by his armpits, and lug him to the entrance of our hut. I smash the door with my heel and move the bits of compacted snow aside. The dogs go crazy as they spot their chief.

I dig our sled out of a snow drift, drag Katvar up unto it, and fetch his furs to cover him. My gaze pauses on the large package that's supposed to stay behind. It contains the ultrasound scanner.

More weight yet, but it might end up saving Katvar's life. I fetch the small machine and rewrap our packages, then tie the frantic dogs to the sled and give them the go signal.

The sled jumps forward. The dogs and I kick up mushy

snow as we race to the aircraft that's only a couple of minutes away. The ice anchor goes in first, then it's unleashing the dogs and tying their lines to the nose gear strut. But they don't want to go where I want them to go. Their bodies point toward Katvar. Balto stands in his harness, yapping. They don't even hear what I'm shouting.

Cursing, I push the sled with Katvar ten, twelve steps ahead of the aircraft to line up the dogs. They pull without me needing to tell them to. But the machine doesn't move.

I run back to the hut and grab my axe, then chip away at the ice that's blocking the wheels and ski. Still nothing. Tears of fury and despair curse down my face. I jam the head of the axe into the ice. Using the axe as a lever, I push at one of the wheels. A creak and the thing begins to move. I wipe snot off my nose and keep pushing, grab the whip that Katvar uses only to tap at his dogs to direct them left or right, and smack the animals' backsides. They yelp and jump, pulling harder. Centimetre by agonising centimetre, the aircraft moves.

When we finally reach Katvar, my throat burns from cursing.

'You okay?' I ask.

His eyes tremble in their sockets. He blinks at me sluggishly and works his jaw as though to speak.

'Hang in there. We're nearly ready to take off,' I lie.

I pull him farther out, baiting his dogs. My underwear is soaked and plastered to my skin, my arms hurt from hacking and pushing, from whipping the dogs. My legs are rubber. I can't give up now. We're so close.

Again, I push Katvar further out, and again the dogs and I pull, push, shout, bark. My knees wobble, my whole body is a wreck, and I have no clue where I'm getting the strength from to move eight hundred kilograms through jumbled ice with only three dogs and my own skeleton.

But we make it. We make it.

Can I have a wheelbarrow-sized serving of buttered string beans, with dumplings, and roasted ham, swimming in its own fat, and — if it's not too much to ask — strawberries for dessert?

I land face first in the snow. Saliva fills my mouth. What the hell was that? Hallucination? Fuck, I hope not. Touching my head, I push myself up. What was I supposed to do next? Right, release the dogs, move Katvar into the machine. Maybe moving him first, shut the door, and then untie the dogs might be better?

I'd be happy with a slice of dry bread, though. Doesn't have to have ham.

I slap my face and get to work. Dragging him to the machine, I try to wake him. We collapse by the door, and I'm openly sobbing now. I've nothing left in me. Moving my fingers is too much, keeping my eyes open is…

'Shut up, Micka!' I scold myself. 'Self-pity won't get you anywhere.'

It can't be helped. I tap Katvar hard on his chest. 'You need to stand up!'

His lids flutter and his eyes don't seem to focus on anything. He reaches out and misses me by a generous measure.

'I'll get you to a hospital. Alta has a hydropower plant, and they'll have a hospital, I'm sure. And good physicians.' I'm babbling on and on, as we crawl up the three steps and into the belly of the aircraft. Breathing heavily, I rest my head on Katvar's chest.

'Get your things, wrap him up, untie the dogs, start the engines,' I mutter to myself. Saying the words helps to make my legs move.

THE BOHEMIAN VILLAGES are at twelve per cent. Three per

cent more than a few days ago. I squeeze my ass into the flimsy hammock seat I fashioned from twine and strips of reindeer skin. There are no buckles. A hard landing could kill us.

No time to think about that.

I start the engines. Their sputtering drowns out the barking and yapping of the dogs. Automatic takeoff procedure is engaged; I have to force myself *not* to grab the yoke. I want to pull at it with all my might. Make it race toward the sun and then, Alta. And I'm scared as all hell of relinquishing control to a computer.

On a display I watch numbers and letters appear. Temperature, wind force, direction. Precipitation and ISO intensity.

"Battery charge critical," it tells me.

No kidding.

"Fuel conservation activated."

'Why wasn't *that* in your manual?' I squeak. But the computer won't enlighten me. Bitch.

"Flaps: 5°. Calculating required takeoff distance."

I stuff an index finger into my mouth and chew on the nail.

"1340 meters takeoff distance. Proceed with fuel conservation takeoff? Yes (recommended) / No"

I tap *yes*, because, duh. The ice is smooth and we have a shitload of space. Vibrations rattle the plane and I'm sweating again. Rubbing my palms on my thighs, I cast a quick glance over my shoulder. A small cloud of breath hovers over Katvar's mouth. I tear my attention back to the controls. We're speeding up. The bohemian villages are at nine per cent.

Fuck.

"Battery charge critical."

My hand is poised above the yoke. I can't *not* do

anything. Can't let a machine decide whether or not we're going to kick the bucket.

The wheels detach from the ice. We're climbing! I nearly piss my pants laughing. But it's too early to feel relieved. The hard part is happening now. We're up in the air and the batteries are at…four per cent.

"Battery charge critical."

'Shut the fuck up! I'm not blind!'

The cloud cover is near. So near. One millimetre from the yoke, I curl my fingers to a fist.

That's when the bleeping concert of doom begins. "Battery charge critical. Battery charge critical."

At three per cent, I grab the yoke and pull. The engines whine. The clouds swallow us.

Everything bleeps and flashes red, urging me to initiate emergency landing procedure immediately.

I press "override."

One per cent.

We are floating in white cotton.

Behind me, Katvar begins to scream.

Nine

At our current speed and headwind, it will take an hour to reach the Norwegian coast. Never has an hour been so agonisingly long. It feels like a lifetime. Excursions to the cockpit to check course and refuelling procedure are kept to a minimum. I hold Katvar gently as he claws at me. Tranquillise him with morphine when he hyperventilates. I slap his cheeks and massage his limbs when the morphine slows his breathing too much.

His eyes flutter open. He tries a smile and my heart soars. I kiss his lips. That's when he starts seizing. His face, his whole body contorts in a paroxysm.

I know seizures. My brother had them. Died from one. The term "brain damage" hits my mind like a brick, carrying flavours of unripe raspberries and green leaves to my palate.

I guess I've known for days. I just…never *wanted* to know.

That's when I do something I'd never have dreamed in less dire circumstances: I switch on the emergency comm and broadcast our position. 'Mayday, mayday! Small solar aircraft needs to… I'm… I… Fuck! Whoever is listening, I need a doctor. My friend has a head injury and… He's having seizures. I think he's dying! I need a—'

'Small solar aircraft, this is Alta tower. What's your position?' a voice as furry as a bear's butthole answers.

A sob of relief burst from my mouth. 'About fifty kilometres north of Alta.'

'Small solar aircraft, can you specify?'

'My GPS isn't working!' I blurt out, trying to sound surprised at the fact.

'Please squawk ident.'

'You want me to…squawk?'

He clears his throat. 'Your injured friend is the pilot of this plane?'

Brilliant solution! I don't even have to think about it before saying, 'Yes! I have no idea what I'm doing, so…'

'Copy that,' the bastard says cooly. 'Please press the ident button on your transponder.'

I find it and jab it with my thumb.

A long moment later, he says, 'Small solar aircraft, we have you on our radar. Turn right to one niner zero. Descend to three thousand four hundred. Speed one seven zero.'

For a second, I'm speechless. 'Can you repeat that in English?'

'Turn to the right until your compass shows one hundred ninety degrees. Slow down to one hundred seventy knots, and go down to three thousand four hundred feet altitude.' Spoken like he's announcing the weather.

As I fumble with the yoke, my shitty hammock seat swings and nearly tips me out, but after several minutes Bear Butt says, 'Looking good. Hold that. You said your pilot is injured. May I ask your names and where you're from?'

In my panic, I almost blurt out "Svalbard." But nothing good can come from everyone on the frequency knowing it's Katvar and me who blew up the satellite network. 'We're coming from Greenland. There was an attack. The BSA shot my Sequencer. His name is Ben. I'm his apprentice, Sandra. A bullet grazed his head and I think something inside is damaged. He's having seizures. He needs a doctor. Can you get us a doctor? We can...pay.'

There's silence. Seconds tick by. I chew the inside of my cheeks to shreds. A long time ago, Sandra was my lover for one night. I'd almost forgotten her. Ben, though... Ben was my friend. The BSA shot down his solar plane, burning him and his apprentice Yi-Ting alive. And Yi-Ting... I can't even think of her name without pain burrowing into my stomach.

'Our hospital is full. We can't help your friend. I'm sorry.' He sounds like he really *is* sorry.

'If you save his life, you can have my ultrasound scanner. It's in top condition and can save a lot of lives.' My voice breaks and I hate myself for showing weakness.

More silence on the other end. Then, 'I'll talk to someone,' and with a crackle, the connection breaks off. I blink.

The machine skims over a blanket of clouds. I glance over at the controls to make sure I'm not missing some red warning light telling me I've screwed up, then pull my arse from the hammock seat and move back to Katvar.

I don't know if my heart can break any further. His face is chalky, his eyes shut. Half his body is oddly twisted in a convulsion. The morphine is used up. All I can do is place my hands on his cheeks and kiss him softly, making promises that I can't keep. I doubt he hears them.

'Sandra, this is Alta tower. One of our physicians has agreed to take a look at your friend. He suspects brain herniation and suggests you lose altitude ASAP to decrease intracranial pressure. Descend to one thousand. Speed niner zero. As soon as you see us, switch over to automatic landing procedure.'

I can't wait to get this machine on the ground, so I do as Bear Butt says, twisting my neck to keep one eye at the controls and the approaching city, and the other on Katvar.

But then I have to tear my attention away from him to focus on the landing.

'We have a visual,' crackles through the radio. 'Looking good.'

There's one landing strip that's been cleared of ice and snow. I muddle around for ages to line up the machine, then let go of the yoke. The computer modifies speed and flaps. It's eerie to watch. Learning to fly will be high on my to-do list if…*when* Katvar is better.

With a whomp and a screech, we touch down. I strain my eyes to spot people but see no one. The machine slows to a crawl, then stops. The place is deserted. It gives me the creeps.

'Please wait for permission to leave the aircraft,' sounds from the radio.

'I'm sorry, what? My friend is dying—'

'Security is approaching. Wait for permission.'

'The fuck I will!'

'If you open the door without our permission, you will be shot. Stay in the aircraft.'

'You 54 kbit ass! You…cheating shit bucket!' I extract myself from my hanging seat and almost face plant the floor. Scrambling to Katvar, I see that he's stopped seizing and his tense side has relaxed a little.

But he's unconscious.

I stand and peek through a window to find four men approaching in a run, their assault rifles pressed to their chests, muzzles down. The good thing is, they don't look like the BSA. But they don't look like Sequencers, either.

Flicking off the safety of my pistol, I leap back to the cockpit. Bohemian villages are at twelve per cent. Exactly where we started. Patches of sunlight dapple the airstrip. I could just take off again and—

'Sandra, this is Alta tower. Security is positioned at the door, a physician is awaiting your friend. You are now allowed to exit.'

I sink to my knees and curl my hand around Katvar's jaw. If I open this door, we both might be dead in seconds. If I take off, he'll die, and that's a given. Inhaling a steadying breath, I return to the cockpit and pick up the radio. 'I don't see a physician.'

'He's waiting in the hangar.'

'All I see are four armed men, Mr. Turd Burglar. I'm not opening this door until the physician has moved his arse to my friend and looked at him.'

'Negative. If you want treatment for your friend, you'll have to remove all weapons from your person, open the door, and allow security to enter.'

Bear Butt is fucking us over.

My hand hovers over the engine controls. One flick is all it takes to leave. But where to go? Tromsø is what — two, three hundred kilometres away? I could take off and find another doctor to treat Katvar. I could fly low so as not to make it worse for him and… Shit, I can't. I still need the sun to refuel the machine. And Katvar's horribly still form tells me he has no time for this crap.

Swallowing, I approach the door, and shout, 'I am coming out now.'

With a soft hiss, the door opens. A muzzle is in my face the same instant I'm pointing my pistol at a…woman? Her stance and fluid movements tell me she's not one to fuck with. Her hair is shorn to her skull where her fur hood droops. From afar I took her for a man, but her eyes, mouth and cheekbones tell a different story. Definitely *not* BSA.

Her gaze doesn't waver as she says, 'If you want to live, lower your gun.'

Meeting someone down the barrel of a gun doesn't make for pleasant conversations.

'Promise you'll save him.' I tip my chin in Katvar's direction.

'Do I look like a physician to you?' she bites out.

'What do I know? Get me a doctor and I'll lower my weapon.'

'You are in no position to negotiate. I'll count to three, then I will fire. One…'

I don't move a muscle.

'Two…'

'If he dies, I'll kill you.' I flip the gun in my hand, and hold it out with two fingers. She snatches it faster than I can curse, steps back and waves at me to hop down to the tarmac. Three men clamber up into the aircraft. Two drag Katvar out roughly by his armpits, the third grabs the ultrasound scanner.

I'm going to kill Bear Butt.

Ten

As we run toward the hangar, I cut a quick glance over my shoulder. The man behind Female Killer Machine is carrying the ultrasound scanner, the other two…are searching the sky? Everyone seems on high alert. From the corners of my vision, I see another man hopping into our solar plane and moving it off the landing strip. This place is an anthill — you throw a few bread crumbs on it and the goodies are carried away faster than you can say, "You're welcome, creeps."

The hangar gate opens silently and I'm pushed through. Katvar's boots scrape on the concrete. His head hangs low. Blood from his gunshot wound is beginning to seep through the bandage.

Several steps into the hangar, I put on the brakes, ignoring the shove of the gun between my shoulder blades.

'I need to check his breathing! You're being too rough with him!'

'I've got it,' someone behind me answers. A new guy. We must have passed him on the way in.

The woman steps back from me, keeping her gun trained on my centre mass. 'I told you to *wait* until we searched them.' She sounds annoyed. As if she's his bodyguard and he never listens to her warnings. I make a mental note to exploit this weak link if Katvar and I need to disappear quickly.

The guy doesn't reply as he kneels next to Katvar, pulls his lids apart and shifts a small beam of light in and out of his face. He unwraps the bandage, muttering, 'Tangential gunshot wound. You said you have an ultrasound— Aw, thanks, mate.'

The scanner is handed to the new guy, who switches it on and presses the gel pillow to Katvar's wound. 'Bullet didn't breach the skull.' Then he moves it to the opposite side of Katvar's head. 'Herniation of the brain. As I thought. Hand me my bag.'

I creep closer, but Female Killer Machine stops me.

'The bleeding was on the other side of his head?' I ask.

'Yes. It's quite common.'

I want to smack my head against something hard. Studying basic emergency medicine goes on my to-do list.

The physician slides a needle into Katvar's elbow bend and attaches a tube and an IV bottle. He looks up at me and says, 'He's getting hypertonic saline to decrease the pressure in his brain. That's all I can do at the moment.'

My gaze skitters to the bottle. "23.4% NaCl" it reads. 'You are giving him salt?'

'Yes. It's simple but effective.' He looks at a watch on his wrist. I've never seen anyone with a wrist watch before, but maybe doctors need them?

'Three minutes. The tension in his arm is lessening. See?' he says.

'It's…helping?' I don't dare hope. Is that why the over-salted stew made Katvar's headache better?

'For now, but that doesn't mean he'll survive.' He looks up at his "mate" and tells him that the patient can now be moved to the hospital. 'You, too,' he says to me.

Female Killer Machine protests, but Physician Guy gets the last word. I keep my mouth shut because I want to go where Katvar goes, and to find out if Physician Guy's soft side can be exploited. If it can…well, I'm not going to hesitate.

We exit the hangar and rush into a squat building. Its insides are crumbling. Strange metal stairs with teeth-like steps — half of them missing or loose — connect to a lower level. Tiny shrubs and lichen have crept through cracks in the structure; crooked miniature birches have managed to grab onto larger fissures. Icy wind blows through empty window and door frames. I stumble through an opening, knees weak, mind mushy. Coming down from the high of danger has never been my favourite.

Again, the woman jabs her rifle into my back. Physician Guy's "mate" is holding a door open for us. I must be having some kind of blackout because I can't recall what happened between the broken-down airport building and this door. I guess I need a break. Physician Guy is saying something that sounds like a drawn-out underwater fart.

Then the floor warps and is yanked from under my feet.

GREEN PAINT PEELS off the ceiling. Lights flicker. My head hurts. The wall touching my shoulder is the brownish-grey of post-war concrete. Someone nearby is screaming. My body seems buried under sacks of grain, or whatever some asshole might have thrown over me. Blinking, I gaze down to my boots. Only my clothes are covering me. No other weight.

Still, I feel crushed.

The floor under my butt is hard and cold. My anorak is tucked under my torso, the pullover under my head. I find my sleeve rolled up and a needle in my elbow bend, right were my 1/2986 scar is. That's what's left of humanity: the 2986th part of ten billion. I wonder if that number is right, or if we're still going downhill since the last count. Or if anyone is even bothering to count us.

My eyes follow the tube attached to the needle to find two bottles hanging upside down in a net and labelled "Ringer" and "Glucose." Glucose sounds delicious. Wish I could taste its sweetness on my parched tongue. Ringer sounds like it's supposed to wake me from my daze. I doubt it, though. Fighting dizziness, I push myself up on my butt, press my back to a cold wall, and draw my legs up to my chest.

There are more patients filling this corridor, all lying on their backs or curled up on their sides. Most are sleeping or unconscious, some with IVs like mine. Looks like Ringer is the magic solution to all your health problems. Even for the guy with a bloody stump instead of a lower leg. I squint at his bluish face. Is he…dead?

'Hello?' I try. My voice sounds weird. Like I haven't used it in a long time. 'I need a doctor here.'

A few heads turn in my direction. People mutter in a language I don't understand.

'It's not your turn, chicken breast!' A man with a greasy beard covering much of his face and a heavy Norwegian or Swedish accent hollers from five patients down. 'I was here before you.' For emphasis, he taps gnarled fingers against the bloody bandage that covers his chest.

''Kay,' I answer and take a hard look at the guy with one and a half legs. Seems like he won't need a doctor, judging from his colour and his unmoving ribcage.

So that's why Bear Butt said the hospital was full. It's not only full, it's stuffed to the eyeballs.

'Why all the injured people?' I ask Greasy Beard.

'Which hole in this goddamned earth did *you* crawl from?'

'Greenland.' That's when I realise Female Killer Machine isn't here pointing a gun at me. Strange. But who am I to complain?

'That explains it, I guess.' Greasy Beard coughs. The bandage around his chest darkens. 'The BSA attacked Tromsø a week ago. Heavy losses on both sides. Alta sent their only aircraft. A fat antique that's still running on some old-fashioned jet fuel. Or…was. Fuel's gone now. But they got us out. They got us out.' His voice is wet and bubbly.

'The BSA took Tromsø?'

He grunts an affirmative noise.

Fuck. We probably made the BSA a bit angry what with blowing up their satellite network and all. But they must have been planning the attack on Tromsø long before that.

'Did the Sequencers come to help?' I ask, eyeing a large double door through which occasional screams are coming.

Greasy Beard chokes on a mouthful of air, and cackles like an axe chopping wood.

I'm getting worried my stupid questions might kill him.

'There was a man brought in with me. Any idea where he is?'

'Dark hair, green face, leaky head?'

I nod.

'The boy is in the operating room.' Greasy Beard waggles his fingers in the direction of the double door.

I push myself to my feet, contemplating whether to rip out the IV or just unhook the bottles from the nail in the wall and carry them with me. Might need both my hands, though. 'Who's screaming in there?' It's not Katvar's voice, that much is clear.

'Whoever they're cutting up.' He makes it sound as if it's as obvious as gravity and I'm stupid to even ask.

My hand drops to where I strapped my knife to my hip but I come up empty. Assholes. I pull the needle from my arm and step over several people to reach the double door. It groans as if it's about to come off its hinges when I push it open.

Three people in worn aprons of different colours stand around a fourth, who lies on a rickety table, a piece of leather in her mouth, her forehead slick with sweat. Four gloved hands poke around in a large wound on the woman's thigh.

'Closing up now,' one man mutters through a handkerchief tied around his mouth and nose.

My gaze scans the floor. The concrete shows in patches where its plastic coating has been worn off by centuries of boot traffic. Blood splatters around the table, old and new. Patients lining the walls. My heart stops when I spot Katvar. His eyes are shut, his mouth slack, head covered in bandages. I rush to his side, nearly knocking over a cracked plastic chair that has surgical tools spread on its seat.

I check his breathing and heartbeat. Finding both, I press a sob into his chest.

'Don't move him,' a female voice sounds from behind me. 'His head needs to remain elevated to facilitate drainage.'

I check the bunched up coat under his head, then make sure he can't roll off it easily. I sit on my haunches to take in the physicians. They're still operating on the woman, who's chomping away on her leather gag. Two of them are male — sewing layer upon layer of tissue shut; the other is a female, watching. Physician Guy isn't here.

'Will he make it?' I ask.

'Maybe,' she says, not taking her eyes off her patient on the operating table. 'Do you have antibiotics and painkillers in your plane?'

'I have a MedKit. But no antibiotics or painkillers.' I don't tell her that I've used up all the morphine on Katvar, just as she doesn't tell me the plane has already been searched. That's what I would have done, anyway.

She doesn't reply, just nails me a brief, steely gaze.

Her two colleagues start bandaging the woman. One of them speaks in Norwegian or Swedish. Or maybe Dutch. I have no idea. The woman on the table removes the gag from her mouth with feeble fingers and curses at him. Then her arm drops like a rock, her head lolls.

The woman who was talking to me says something about the unconscious woman and checks her pulse.

'Is she going to be okay?'

'She isn't going to lose her leg, if that's what you mean.'

They carefully lift her from the table and lay her down next to another patient.

'Doesn't look like one of your fancy Sequencer hospitals, does it.' The female physician says. There's no judgement in her voice, only resignation.

I shrug. 'I've never seen one. Have you?'

71

She nods once before checking on a man with a thick, fresh bandage around his head. She mutters to him and places a hand over one of his eyes, then the other. 'Thanks for the ultrasound scanner. It has already saved two lives.' She points her chin at the man in front of her, and then at Katvar.

'Can you tell if…' No, she already said "maybe" when I asked before if he'd make it. 'Can you tell me anything?'

'We had to place an emergency drainage. The next twenty-four hours will tell if he survives. But we have no time to monitor him. Feel free to volunteer.'

Two men are hoisting another patient onto the table. A teenage girl who's eyeing the surgical tools with horror.

'What kind of emergency…drainage?' I ask.

The girl on the table lifts her head and spits in broken English, 'They drilled a hole in his head. But something was wrong with him. His screams were weird.'

Eleven

'Y ou bitch did *what?*' I curl my hands to fists, ready for bloodshed.

'He was bleeding inside his skull. The pressure on his brain needed to be lowered. Creating an opening usually does that. Got a better idea?' The female physician doesn't even look at me.

'But...' I don't have a better idea. My hand gently cups Katvar's cheek and I wonder if he's ever going to be okay again. I say as much.

'Look, we have another forty or fifty patients out there. You aren't injured and you're wasting my time. Leave, or start being useful.'

The teenage girl on the operating table fires words at the physicians, gestures at me and squares her chin. She wants me to piss off.

Like I care.

The woman flicks a brief glance at me. 'Find one of the nurses and tell them I said you are to feed and wash the patients.'

'What about Katvar? He…needs to eat. Hasn't eaten for days.' Fuck. I realise my blunder the moment I speak his name. But none of the physicians seems puzzled. Maybe they weren't told his fake name. Not important when you're drilling a hole in someone's head or cutting a leg off, is it?

'What do you think the IV is for? Now…' She pulls in a deep breath. The handkerchief covering her nose and mouth dimples. 'Get out of here, or I'll make you.' She touches the side of her thigh as though there's a gun hidden under her apron.

Maybe there is.

I clear my throat, mutter my thanks, and leave.

THE HOSPITAL IS A MAZE. When you're starved and exhausted, your trek through its long corridors seems without end. Eventually, I find a nurse elbow-deep in a bucket of soap water. She's scrubbing the floor of another operating room. She tosses me a brush when I ask if I can help. I kneel and get to work.

When spots dance in my vision and I keep dropping the brush, she scolds me and drags me two floors down, then through an empty eating hall and into a large kitchen. She plops me on a wooden crate and scoops cooked grain, meat, and an extra dollop of lard into a bowl.

I put my cheek on my palm, elbow on my thigh, and spoon food into my mouth. It's all I can do not to drop my face into the bowl. There's so much fat in this, I could die of happiness. She doesn't seem disturbed by my sloppy eating, or the smacking and moaning and grunting noises I'm making.

Then it's back to scrubbing floors, haphazardly washing patients scheduled for surgery as well as those who are so bad off they can't move a limb. My heart wants to be where Katvar is, but my mind needs all the available intel on the people of Alta, and why they sent their only aircraft to Tromsø and used up all the fuel they had. Why the BSA wants Tromsø, why the Sequencers didn't come, and most of all — what people make of all the burning satellites that are still painting streaks of fire on the sky.

Unfortunately, my nurse is reticent. She's more into scrubbing than talking. And she won't let me interrogate the patients.

IT'S GROWING dark when the staff make their way down to the eating hall. The general mood is sombre, eroded. I catch a word here and there about lives lost in the ongoing battle of Tromsø.

The female physician who attended Katvar enters with one of her two male colleagues. Spotting me, she veers in my direction and slides into the chair opposite me. Black shadows loom beneath her eyes and there's a red line where the edge of her handkerchief mask has dug into her cheeks. Her hair is dirty blonde, her eyes bright blue and flat with fatigue.

'If I told you your plane was ready to take off, would you be able to fly back to where you came from and get medical supplies?' she asks.

'There's not much, but I guess it's possible.'

Her hand that's moving a spoonful of food to her mouth pauses for a moment. 'What could you get us?'

'An MIT FireScope and a defibrillator. The MedKit you have already, I assume.'

She sputters. 'A FireScope and a defibrillator?' Her voice carries through the hall and the clonking and chattering grows a bit quieter. But that might just be my imagination.

She leans forward, blinks. 'Really? That would... We could diagnose disease, we could... Are you *sure* you can get us those things?'

'Y-yes.'

She narrows her eyes. 'But?'

'How's my friend?'

'Stable.'

'Like...he's going to make it? No brain damage?' I feel my face pull into a grin.

'Like stable. He's unconscious, but his vital signs are looking good. Anything else is guesswork. Now, about those supplies—'

'How do you keep up communication with Tromsø? All the satellite comms...seem to be down.'

She snorts. A fleck of meat lands on the table. She wipes it away and shakes her head. 'You Sequencers are a spoiled lot. Never heard of radio?'

'Right.' Feeling stupid, I drop my head to empty my bowl.

'So... About those *things*. When can you get them?'

'I'm not going without my friend. It has to wait until he's recovered.'

'Bullshit.'

'He's the pilot.'

She leans so close to my face, I can see the small lines of dark blue that fan though her irises. 'You mean *Katvar,* who's supposed to be *Ben?*' As she leans back, there's no smile, no triumph in her expression. 'The Brothers and

Sisters of the Apocalypse have begun to drop leaflets from a solar plane much like yours. They are targeting cities. Tromsø, Narvik, Bodø. And Alta. Do you know what they're spreading?'

She makes it sound like I *should* know. 'You think I'm with them?'

Ignoring my question, she continues. 'God punishes humanity by sending his four horsemen of the apocalypse — Pestilence, War, Famine, and Death. First, Pestilence, or if you will, the Great Pandemics. Then, War — the World Wars. Next in line, Famine — basically everyone who survived the wars has spent their shitty lives starving. And now, *now* comes Death. That's what the BSA believe they've been chosen for. By God. That's what they're saying in those leaflets.'

She empties her bowl and sets it down. 'And where do you fit in?'

STANDING BY A WINDOW, I gaze out onto the fjord, the black silhouettes of the mountains, the water glimmering faintly in the night. The wind is a constant here. The cold. The trees have learned to stay hunched. Not the people, though, it seems.

I left the female physician — who still hasn't told me her name, but then, I haven't told her mine, either — where she sat. I need a minute to myself to digest what she's told me.

Erik's propaganda is brilliant. I have to give him that. All during the Great Pandemics and the World Wars, religious fundamentalists gave everyone an earful on how angry God was with humanity, and that the apocalypse was here. They hollered it from every street corner, and painted it on every building. They've been using it to justify their killing and maiming and raping. Because they've been *ordained* to.

And now, even though religion's been banned, or at least frowned upon, everyone still remembers the four horsemen of the apocalypse. It's what parents tell their kids, and teachers tell their pupils — that people used the tale of the four horsemen to justify endless suffering and death.

Every child learns from a young age that religion has been the excuse for murder, abduction, torture, and genocide by countless generations. And that's what Erik is using now — that deep-rooted fear.

He doesn't need to drop bombs to strike terror into the hearts of people. That would be a waste of good explosives. No, dropping pieces of paper with a dark fairy tale on them is enough.

Cursing, I push at the nearest door and walk into the teeth of the wind.

Twelve

Pretending I'm on a casual walk and not recon, I pull my fur hood over my head, stuff my hands into my pockets and saunter around the hospital building. Three wings, three storeys. A lot of open space, and no cover taller than knee-high shrubs. Still, in the dark, as long as no one is using night vision, this could even work. But Katvar would have to be able to walk, or better yet, run.

Fuck, I wish I had my rifle on me. On the other hand, if I'd brought it from Bear Island, it would now be Female Killer Machine's toy.

And I'd made a mistake telling Bear Butt we're Sequencers from Greenland. With the BSA attacking Tromsø, the *real* Sequencers can't be far. And if they hear that two Sequencers from Greenland have just landed a solar plane in Alta, they'll grow suspicious, because they've just lost a solar plane on Svalbard. They probably even watched me kill their men, and feed one of them to our dogs. And because Greenland is — or was until a few weeks ago — BSA territory. I doubt any Sequencer has voluntarily set foot on Greenland in the past decade and lived to tell the tale.

If shit hits the fan, Katvar and I will need an escape route. Better two or three, with plenty of hideouts along the way.

Puffing clouds of condensation, I turn into Alta's empty streets. You can't even call them streets, really. Where snow has been pushed aside, the northern lights skitter over asphalt pulverised by countless freeze-thaw cycles, revealing stretches of naked rock. Flat buildings are coated in withered plaster, peeling paint, lichen, and moss. The houses look tired. As if holding a roof over people's heads is exhausting enough, let alone providing a cosy place anyone would want to call home. Many of the broken windowpanes have been replaced by thick reindeer skins. Light is leaking around their furry edges. Nature has taken over.

I like it better that way.

As I scan for bashed in basement windows, abandoned apartments, and storage rooms, I consider contacting the Sequencers. I used to be one of them. We're still on the same side, want the same thing: to get rid of the BSA. But I would have to prove that I never betrayed them.

Flavours of cold metal bite the back of my mouth as memories of the battle of Taiwan hit me full force. All the lives lost: Yi-Ting, Ben. Runner. And Kat.

My boots scuff across frozen gravel. I come to a halt. What precisely did Kat tell her contacts about Erik and his ability to manipulate the Sequencers' satellite feed? She never let us know. And she was so ready to blame me for all that went wrong.

What if...

I grow hot.

Kat was the communications specialist for our small force on Taiwan. She was openly distrustful of me from the moment she learned that Erik — head of the BSA — was my father. Or sire. Or whatever one calls a sperm provider who never even bothered to say hi.

The first time I saw that man's face was when Kat pulled up the visual from Ben and Yi-Ting's recognisance flight over Taiwan's BSA camp. My first thought was, "So that's where I've got my stupid orange hair from."

And then I'd wanted to puke. The man who had managed to pull factions of extremists, rapists, and murderers into one organised group was my own father? What an epic fuckuppery.

But what if Kat never did inform her contacts of Runner and my suspicions: that Erik, a former Sequencer and satellite specialist, was both the leader of the BSA, and the one who gave the BSA access to and control over the global satellite network? The network the Sequencers believed to be exclusively their own?

What if she told her contacts her own theory: that Erik had switched sides, and that I — his daughter — had showed up on that same island to join my father and get my friends killed?

Squeezing my eyes shut, I pull in a deep breath. So much can happen, and I have to plan for every eventuality, have to guess what all those eventualities might be. Can we expect protection from anyone here? I shake my head. First rule of survival: Never expect help. Second rule: Never trust strangers.

If the Sequencers should hear that two of their own

were in Alta, without assignment, would they send someone to check?

Yes, definitely.

We'll have to get out of here as soon as Katvar is better. Get our aircraft, fly back to Bear Island, fetch our stuff. And then we're off to nowhere. The Sequencers can kiss our imaginary asses.

WITH A MAP of our immediate surroundings in my head, I make my way back to the hospital in search of Katvar.

I find him on the second floor, not far from the operating room. He's in a small room with eight other people. A narrow aisle cuts through makeshift beds of reindeer skins. A greenish glint from the northern lights reflects off a row of IV bottles hanging upside down on the wall. I shut the door and let my eyes adjust to sudden darkness, then tiptoe around sleeping bodies to kneel next to Katvar. Touching my fingers to his cheek, I feel his warmth. Only then do I dare check his pulse and breathing.

The thrum of his heart echoes mine.

He's alive.

My hands slide to his neck, and down his arms to his hands, checking his temperature. His fingers are a bit cold, so I spread my anorak over him and sneak under his furs, gently wrapping my body around his to keep him warm, taking care not to jostle his other arm with the IV in it. With my hand on his chest — on the slow and steady beat of his heart — peace settles into me. Katvar has food, shelter, and medical care. He will be fine. He *has* to be.

My gaze rests on his profile that's softly illuminated by northern lights. The scruff on his jaw has grown longer than he finds comfortable. If I can find a sharp knife, I'll shave him tomorrow.

'You will be okay,' I whisper. 'You are brave and strong.'

Doubt sneaks in. What if he's sustained brain damage? Would he *want* to live? What if he never wakes up?

My eyes begin to burn. I can't think of that now. I *can't*. 'Rest, my love. I'm here. You are safe. I'm not leaving you.'

Fear constricts my throat. How can he eat anything if he's not waking up? He can't live off IVs alone, can he? Clenching my jaw, I get a grip on myself.

'I miss you,' I say softly and kiss his cheek, the corner of his mouth, his lips. 'Don't leave me yet.'

There's a small movement of his lips, like a butterfly beating its wings against my mouth. I kiss him again, cautiously, hoping he'll kiss me back, even just a tiny bit. But there's nothing. No sign of life but his breath feathering my skin, his heart beating under my hand.

A tear slips from my lashes onto his cheek. I wipe the moisture away and press my face to his shoulder. 'It's okay. You need to sleep. I'll sleep a bit, too. Right here. I'll keep you warm. Don't leave without me.'

DAWN CREEPS THROUGH A WINDOW. Tape criss-crosses cracked panes, holding the pieces together. My gaze searches Katvar's face for signs of improvement, for any indication that he'll wake up and be healthy.

Sounds seep through the door. Voices and footfalls.

I catch small bits of conversation, but can't make anything of it. Probably doctors or nurses talking about patients. Then I hear a man's voice, sharp and annoyed, 'I've just told you — we didn't send anyone to Greenland!'

Someone answers but I don't understand the words. A door opens not far from our room. Heart in my mouth, I look at Katvar, knowing this is goodbye. Cupping his face in my hands, I brush a kiss to his lips and whisper, 'You are safe. They want me, not you. I'll lead them away. And… and I swear I'll come back. I'll come back for you. I swear it on my life.'

I peel myself from the bed and pick up my anorak. There's nothing on him now that connects him to me. Except…the drive. It's useless now. Just a trinket. But I can't risk leaving it on Katvar or taking it with me. If they find it on us, it'll prove what we did. They have no reason to search him as long as they don't suspect him. Or do they? Would they search everyone in this room? The whole hospital?

I slip the leather string with the drive from around his neck, unsure where to hide it. I step to the window. There's no handle to open it. I run my fingers around its frame. Shit. The thing is screwed shut.

The thump of heavy boots on concrete is approaching quickly. Ten seconds until they'll open this door and find me. I scan the patients in the room. All men. One of them lies slack-mouthed in a puddle of bloody froth — Greasy Beard. I climb over another patient, yank at a corner of Greasy Beard's blanket and sneak in next to him. I push the drive far under his back, then rub and pinch my skin around my eyes, hard.

The door swings open.

I press my face onto Greasy Beard's chest and squeeze out a heart-wrenching sob. I make my shoulders shake. Make my fingers rake through the man's filthy hair. Make myself not look at Katvar one last time.

I'll come back for you.

'What happened here?' That's Physician Guy's voice.

Producing a hiccup, I cry, 'He died!'

A hand settles on my shoulder and squeezes softly.

'I'm…' Physician Guy pauses. He knows I'm lying. He knows this is not the injured man he examined in the hangar. 'I'm sorry for your loss,' he says then, and I can't believe he has. I can't believe he's lied for me. For Katvar.

'Thank you,' I whisper, and mean it.

'Someone wants to see you.' He makes his voice sound light, but we both know it's for show.

Nodding, I stand and face two men, their assault rifles casually slung over their shoulders. One of them walks up to Greasy Beard and frowns down at the dead man. 'What's his name?'

'Ben. I'm Sandra.'

He tilts his head at me. 'We heard you flew in from Greenland?'

I give him a nod.

'Mike?' the other Sequencer says. I can hear it in his voice. He's recognising my face.

'We don't know of any assignment on Greenland,' Mike says.

The other guy pulls out his SatPad and logs in.

I kneel and cradle Greasy Beard's cold hand in mine. His fingers are stiff. 'He said that's where we have to go. Something about…' I look up at Mike, trying to ignore the other Sequencer's frantic tapping on the SatPad's screen. 'Something about the Espionage Unit.'

Mike's face grows cold. So he knows about the Espionage Unit — a unit that's not even supposed to exist. Strange, given the Sequencers' constant fight with the BSA. I'm sure each organisation has long infiltrated the other.

'Mike.' The other Sequencer waves him over. They stare at the SatPad for a moment, then at me.

I look at Greasy Beard and imagine it's Katvar's face

I'm seeing. I can't allow myself to look at him now. It hurts not to.

A muzzle meets my temple. 'Mickaela Capra, you are arrested for treason and murder.'

'Whoever gave you that information lied.'

To no one's surprise, they ignore my statement. 'The Council wants you for interrogation,' Mike says.

I can't wait to get them away from Katvar, but I'm aware of Physician Guy standing just behind me. He might be getting doubts now that he's heard "murder" and "treason." But I'm depending on him to keep Katvar safe, and so I say, 'You must be BSA, then.'

Mike blinks slowly, then bursts out a bark of laughter. A fleck of spittle hits the floor. 'We're Sequencers.'

'Funny that it's *you* arresting me when it's the BSA I betrayed. I was their prisoner for two years. When I fled, I butchered their second in command. Do you want to arrest me for that?'

Physician Guy must have stopped breathing, because I don't hear him making those little huffing noises anymore.

'You are working for the BSA. We have proof.' Everything about Mike's face is blunt. Blunt jaw. Blunt gaze. Blunt nose.

'A woman? Working for a bunch of rapists? Do you even hear what you are saying?' This, too, I say for Physician Guy's ears. As long as he doubts the Sequencers' credibility and motives, Katvar should be relatively safe.

I hope.

'You will come with us now.' The other Sequencer jerks his head toward the door, and bumps his muzzle harder against my skull.

'Don't you give a shit about killing an innocent man? Or what did you plan to do about the physician standing right behind your target? Bend the path of your bullets?'

He angles his gun just a little. As though he can barely bring himself to care about collateral damage.

'I want to say goodbye to my friend,' I lie.

The not-so-blunt Sequencer, let's call him Blondie, has enough of my shit. His jaw muscles bulge. Mike, though, seems completely bored. And that's why I nearly miss the quick movement of his arm.

His fist hits my chin, sending me to the tips of my toes.

Blood spurts from my mouth. Fucking amateurs.

His next punch knocks me out cold.

Part Two

Hell is empty and all the devils are here.

William Shakespeare

Thirteen

Soft clicking is wrapped in the feathery brush of reindeer feet on deep snow. I've never figured out why or even how reindeer click when they move. The animals have flat, cloven hooves that are designed like snowshoes, and when you see them walk, you think they float. There's something serene about them.

It's this soft clicking of their legs that's the only noise defined enough for me to keep track of the number of sleds around me. I'm on one, and there's another behind me. A third took a different route soon after we left Alta. But the swooshing of the sled I'm strapped to and the stinky bag Mike yanked over my head muffle the sounds around me.

I tried to measure the distance we were travelling by counting to one thousand. At each thousand, I'd curl a finger into my hand. At ten thousand and one, I bit one cheek hoping that we wouldn't get much further than two cheeks, because I don't have more than two and can't curl in or tuck up any other body part to keep count.

Turns out, I was worrying about the wrong things. I had to stop counting somewhere around twenty-six thousand when I lost feeling in my fingers. So now I'm listening to reindeer clicks for no other reason than to keep my mind busy and awake enough to know when we add company or split up again.

And to keep panic at bay.

The direction we're heading is a complete mystery to me. I gave up tracking left and right turns, the uphills and downhills. Now it's just me, the foul air in my bag coating my tongue, and the soft sounds of reindeer in snow.

The men who took me don't exchange a word.

WITH A CRASH, the world turns upside down. Fuck, I've slept. My heart seizes as I land belly down in the snow. Half frozen, with hands and feet tied and something heavy on top of me, all I can do is wriggle like a maggot. The thick fabric of the bag is wet with my condensed breath, and it's smashed tight against my face by deep snow.

'Can't...breathe!' I wheeze. My ears begin to screech. My ribcage contracts and my throat burns. Air is scarce in my lungs. My brain can't be tricked into needing only traces of oxygen. Turning my head is agony. Something sharp presses into my neck. *Not like this! Not like this!* my mind hollers. What a pathetic way to die.

The weight on my back shifts, and scrapes a hole into my skin as it's lifted off me.

Someone grabs me and flips me on my back. I'm so done, I can't move a finger. The fucking bag still sticks to my face and sucking through the layers of fabric and mush and frozen condensation is like trying to breathe underwater. My mouth is filled with acid. Not sure if it's bile or the taste of suffocation.

Fingers close around my throat. My body bucks without consulting my brain. Some asshole hits me over the head, but I can't stop seizing.

At last, the bag is yanked off.

I suck in sweet air. Blondie is standing above me. I'm so glad to see him, I cry snot bubbles.

'We can't keep her like this,' I hear Mike grumble.

I want to hug them both. Rolling my eyes, I try to bring Mike into focus as he moves away. He gets something from the other sled. Yes! Dry furs, a bite to eat, and a hot drink would be fucking glorious.

He comes back with a sweater.

My idiotic smile (which I blame solely on oxygen deprivation) dies when he pulls the sweater over my head and leaves it there to blindfold me.

WE KEEP ON DRIVING. Might be twenty kilometres, or a hundred, or five hundred from Alta. With my brain back to near-normal Micka-functionality, I think of my old SatPad sitting in a melting snow cave on Bear Island. Two million books humanity will never get to read if Katvar doesn't recover or I don't make it back there. My body feels forlorn without him. My heart is a hole in my chest.

I wish I knew if he…

No. I can't think of that.

Two million books. Erik must have made several copies of that library. And I'm hundred percent sure he's the only one with access to them. Knowledge is power, that's what he drilled into me over and over again. I wonder where he found the files, or…did he take them from the Sequencers?

I make a mental note to find out whether the Sequencers are keeping valuable knowledge from the people they've vowed to protect.

A snort bursts from my mouth. Mike barks at me to shut it.

Sometimes, my naiveté surprises me. The Sequencers have kept from everyone who and what they really are. Only the Sequencers knew about satellite technology. They could have easily used it to help point people to arable and uncontaminated land, or warn them about the storms and floods that are always moving in. But no. What did they use the global satellite network for?

Warfare.

When I was growing up, Sequencers were like…like legends made flesh. Everyone knew they were protecting us. Cacho, the Sequencer who came by once or twice a year, always carrying his MIT FireScope, would analyse our water and soil for cholera germs. I probably should say: he *pretended* to. Knowing what I know now, he might even have done those tests, but it couldn't have made much sense to search for cholera high up in the mountains in a remote settlement.

My throat clenches. It's still raw from trying to breathe. Could it be that Cacho was only coming by to check on me? He was Erik's mentor. Both were satellite specialists, working not far from where I lived.

No one but the Sequencers knew about that satellite control centre. Until Erik switched sides and transferred all that knowledge to the BSA. Although… I wonder how much Erik actually tells his men.

Knowledge is power. He would give them only as much power as they needed to complete a job he gave them.

My thoughts come to a halt when the sled stops. Pricking my ears, I try to identify the location and time of day. Maybe we're making camp. Maybe we're meeting someone.

For a long time, nothing interesting happens. Both men fumble with their clothes. The sounds of piss hitting snow. A few grunts as they have a snack.

The reindeer are getting nervous. Stomping their feet and huffing. A faint but sharp *zzzing* rising from afar steals my last hope that I'll ever know where I'm being brought. Quickly, the noise grows louder, and a few moments later, a train screeches to a stop. The reindeer tug on the sled and Blondie is shouting. Someone grabs me and tries to make me stand. I tip sideways, bumping into Mike's or Blondie's chest. My legs are frozen stiff. No idea what these guys were expecting.

'Walk,' Blondie barks and thumps my back.

My face hits the snow. At least my landing is soft. 'Can't feel my legs,' I croak.

'No talking!' He grabs my anorak and yanks me up, and half carries, half drags me forward. Something sharp hits my shins. *That* I feel.

'Climb!' he barks.

'But I—'

'I said no talking!' He clouts me over the head. Again I fall forward, but this time my landing isn't soft. I grab at something to pull myself away from him. Not fast enough, though. Blondie slaps my arse, then puts his fucking hands on my waist, and gives me a shove. He enjoys this. I start to doubt he and Mike are Sequencers. That thought alone... The possibility they might be BSA tips me over the edge of this tiny precipice of sanity I've been clawing to these past hours. Panic seizes me and everything else fades. My breath and my heartbeat are a staccato. I think

I'm shrieking, or the world is, I'm not sure. It's not even important. Every fibre of my body screams, *I have to get out of here!*

And out I get, as something hard hits my temple.

I COME to in the semi-darkness of a...room? Cell? The gentle rattling and swaying tell me we're in a train. Clinking comes from my wrists and ankles. Ah, they've chained me. I guess that clarifies any questions I might have concerning the pecking order here.

A pair of boots is the next thing my eyes focus on. A guy — not Blondie or Mike — sits on a chair and observes me. His face reveals nothing. He doesn't even seem to be breathing.

My gaze shifts around the small compartment. A window with nothing behind it but blackness. It must be night. I've been on a twelve-hour journey. Minimum. The floor is grated metal. The walls are an aged plastic imitation of cut wood.

My tongue weasels around in my mouth in the search of saliva. 'Who are you? Where am I?' My questions are a waste of time. I see that in the guy's unmoving expression.

'My organisation values truth above all else,' he begins. 'If you answer my questions truthfully, you'll be released. If you don't answer, or you bend the facts...' He shrugs, letting the statement hang there for a while, hoping to impress me. We stare at each other. Someone outside the room is chewing noisily. The scent of pancakes drifts through a barred hole in the door. My stomach yowls.

The guy smirks. 'Hungry?' Again, he shrugs. 'You are a terrorist. Your life means nothing to us.'

So here's the thing: Erik taught me a shitload about interrogation and torture. Mostly through "practical training." Most interrogators get it backwards, which might not be *precisely* what Erik intended to teach me.

An interrogator's main goal is to get information from a detainee. But very few understand that what they *really* want is communication. For that to happen, they need to listen. But guys like Ice Face here have no clue how to do that because their mind is stuck at, "I know what you did, you fucking terrorist."

Ice Face looks like a run-of-the-mill ready-to-kill-ya interrogator. Maybe that's why he got the job. He believes I'm a terrorist. He walked into this room *knowing* I'm a terrorist. He's soaked to the bone with this belief. He'll be blind and deaf to the truth because it won't fit his mindset. Men like him don't want to hear the facts. They just want to destroy people.

I try to look defeated. It's not difficult, as exhausted as I am. 'Can't… Can't think straight. Am starving.'

'When did Erik Vandemeer first contact you?'

Slowly, I sit up and lean my back against the wall. The chain connecting my ankles to my wrists drags over the grated floor. My fingers tremble harder. I open my mouth and shut it, blink, and let my eyes roll back briefly. 'M'sorry what did you say?' Not all of this is an act. I *am* starving. Did I mention, parched?

'I can destroy your life. I can keep you prisoner until your bones rot. When did Vandemeer decide to destroy our satellite network?'

'He said the Espionage Unit knew,' I lie.

'What was that?'

'Water.'

Ice Face balls a fist. His lids lower a fraction. 'Answer my question!'

I slump forward. Drooling would be a nice effect now, might even convince him I'm nearly unconscious, but my mouth feels like it's stuffed with sand. Not sure when the last time was I drank anything.

Ice Face lunges and slaps me. 'No sleep for you! No answers, no sleep, no food, no water!' He kicks his chair out of the way, and exits the room, leaving me shackled, hands to feet. Someone keeps banging on the grille. Whenever I drift off, the asshole shouts, 'No sleep for you!'

Fourteen

Cavity searches were invented to humiliate, not to actually find anything. I've had three so far. They call it "processing." I call it rape and told them so. They laughed. Told me I don't even know what rape is. And that I'm a terrorist and can't expect to be treated like a person.

It suits them just fine to ignore that I've been a BSA prisoner for two years, that I know rape and torture first hand.

I'm not even sure who "they" are. Either they are wearing some stupid knitted hats pulled down all the way to their chins, with holes for eyes and mouth, or a fucking bag is covering my head. Except for one time when I wore a dirty bucket because I'd puked into the bag when someone kicked my stomach.

Today must be the second or third day on the train, but

I'm not sure. They've tried to keep me awake, tried to starve me, never checking or worried if I'd survive this. I blacked out on day one, and woke up to my first cavity search. They got a bit more careful then, what with my bones razoring under my skin. They started feeding me, even offered sweetened tea. It's like in the fairy tale. Can't remember its title, but there was a witch that fattened up two children, planning to butcher and eat them later. I'm not sure if someone came to save them, or if they ended up in the larder.

No one is coming to save me. Katvar doesn't know where I am. Fuck, *I* don't even know where I am, or where I'm going. And I don't know if Katvar is...

I squeeze my eyes shut and bite my tongue, hard. I will not think about the possibility of the only person who matters in my life *not* being anything but alive and well.

'Aren't you supposed to be the good guys?' I ask Ice Face, who entered my compartment after my empty food bowl was taken away.

'Aren't you supposed to be one of us?'

'Who's *us*?'

He cocks an eyebrow.

I cock mine back at him. 'You are such a clown.'

His pupils narrow to pinpricks, which makes me think of Silas, my second husband. Murderer of my newborn daughter.

I dig my fingers into my thigh to distract from the rising panic. Silas is dead. I ripped out his voice box, watched arterial blood arc away from his body. I gutted him. Made sure he stayed dead.

And yet...

My monster is stirring under my skin. It was born at BSA headquarters, and it dug its claws through the little softness I'd foolishly kept in my heart and mind. It helped me pull through, but asked for a hundred times the terror and rage and savagery I thought I could tolerate. It wasn't a conscious decision to let it come to life. When the only alternative to the loss of your life is the loss of your sanity, you instinctively go for the latter, telling yourself that sanity will come back some sunny day.

Like it's that easy.

If it hadn't been for Katvar, I'd still be a hollow, furious shell of a woman.

Ice Face pulls back his shoulders and rolls his neck. Not in a threatening way. Just like someone stretching his limbs to get started on a job. Like baking bread, ploughing fields, chopping off fingers, or removing eyeballs with a spoon.

'Let us begin very simple. Confirm our information and you'll get a blanket.'

Yep, I'm sleeping on naked metal. Shackled. No blanket, no furs. They took my anorak.

'And the shackles go.' I know he won't do that for me, but I don't want to give the impression I'm easy to bait. A blanket would be awesome, though…

'That's not in my power,' he says.

Aw, poor thing. *Not in his power.* I nod like the obedient prisoner I am. 'Okay. Two questions. Two answers. One nice, thick blanket.'

'Five questions. Five truthful answers.'

I squeeze my eyes shut and suck in a breath. It looks like I'm super excited about a meagre blanket — I am! — but I'm doing this mostly to not blurt, "See, that's how you get a sociopathic interrogator to communicate with you!"

'Okay, shoot.'

'When did Erik Vandermeer first contact you?'

'About two, two and a half years ago, when we were stationed on Taiwan.'

Ice Face stands and leaves the compartment. Just

before he shuts the door, he says, 'We try again tomorrow. Until then: no food.'

Aw shit. Facts don't work on Ice Face. I'll have to keep reminding myself of that. And I really wanted that blanket. 'No problem! I was planning to go on hunger strike anyway what with that "no bed" situation.'

'Excellent,' he says and shuts the door.

I don't like the tone he used. And sure enough, a few moments later, the door opens and two masked guys walk in. One with a funnel and a hose, the other with a bucket. 'You on hunger strike?'

Eying their equipment, I wonder what the hell they intend to do with it. 'I want a blanket. I'm freezing my ass off.'

'You get a blanket when you answer our questions.'

'Not my fault that Ice Face walked out on me.'

One guy turns to the other and says, 'You remember how deep it's supposed to go in?'

'What's supposed to go in?' I ask. The hose looks very suspicious right now. And the funnel. 'What's the hose for?'

'Never seen a stomach tube?' the other guy says, then turns back to the first guy. 'Doc said to be careful not to push it into a lung.'

The fuck? I scoot as far away from them as the small compartment allows. My shoulder blades poke the hard wall behind me.

'I say we give it a try,' guy number one says to number two with a shrug.

I clench my jaw. They'll never get that thing into my mouth. *Never*.

They are taking slows steps toward me, enjoying the look of terror on my face. I curl up, teeth clamped shut, head buried between my arms and wrist-to-ankle chains.

The bastards laugh, slap my head, and walk out,

calling back to me, 'Now you know what's gonna happen if you don't eat when we tell you to.'

I'm trapped in my skin of rage and helplessness. I want my rifle, my knife, my pistol, and a large box of ammo.

Fuck it, I want explosives.

Fifteen

I'm a continual source of entertainment for my guards. Especially now that my journey seems to have ended. That was yesterday, but I can't be sure. I don't remember when I last saw daylight. A bulb is screwed to the wall by the door, flickering.

When they kicked me into my cell, I made the mistake of taking the bag off my head as fast as I could. I wanted to breathe. I felt like I hadn't filled my lungs in ages.

I found myself in an empty concrete box with a drain in the floor and a butcher hook in the ceiling.

They laughed when I pissed my pants.

Most of the time, I try to keep my eyes closed and my arm draped over my face to shut out the spasmodic light.

But the hook and the drain are burned into my mind. You really don't need to put any effort into torturing your detainee with an interior design as subtle as this one. Every sane person with a speck of imagination will paint their own fate in a thousand bloody colours, every hour of the day, every day of the week.

I STINK OF OLD PISS.

I'M FED three times a day. Someone will bang on the door and bark at me to face the wall. It's the only thing they say to me, "Face the wall!"

As soon as I have my back to the door, it will open, and a small, wet splash of mashed oats or mashed potatoes or mashed whatever will hit the floor. Then the door slams shut.

I eat like a dog, I'm chained like dog, sleep like a dog.

ICE FACE HASN'T VISITED YET. He'll probably wait until I stink like a garbage heap, thinking I'm ready to do anything for a bucket of clean water and a sliver of soap. Which brings me to the bucket…

There's a bucket in my cell. The water stinks, but it's the only water I have, so I've been scooping it up in my palms and drinking it.

I use the drain as a toilet, but with my ankles chained to my wrists, it's hard to hit the target. I'm glad I don't have to take a dump yet.

Sixteen

I'm the only prisoner here. All I ever hear are the guards, the gurgling of the drain, and the buzzing of the light bulb.

I miss the howling of the wind. The snow. The white expanse.

But most of all I miss...

No, I can't.

I...can't.

Seventeen

D arkness is relative.

Eighteen

Shivering, I listen to the water that drips off the walls, the ceiling, and my clothes. I've just had the pleasure of taking a shower. Two masked guards hosed off my cell and me. There'd been complaints about the smell, they said. I didn't reply. I was too busy trying not to slip in the wet messes I've made and hit my head on the floor.

Now I'm as cold as this concrete box. And I'm tired of waiting.

I am so fucking tired.

Nineteen

'Face the wall!'

It's not feeding time yet. I wonder what they want from me. I hope it's not another shower. The door creaks open, but the splash of food doesn't come. Instead, someone places something hard on the floor.

'You can turn around now.' That's Ice Face's voice.

I shuffle my back to the wall and sit on my haunches. The chains clink against the floor.

He sits on a chair, cradling a steaming mug in his hands. Scents of barley coffee tickle my nostrils.

'Feels a bit cold in here,' he says.

'What do you want?' I hear myself say. I'm so furious, I could explode. If the asshole offers me a blanket in exchange for five answers, I'm going to kill him. He thinks he's invincible. Why else would he come in here, unaccompanied and unarmed?

'You know what I want.' Noisily, he sips at his hot coffee.

'I don't even know who the fuck you are. You told me you're Sequencers, but you behave like the BSA.'

He shrugs. 'Torture is legal under martial law.'

'The BSA have lots of great excuses, too.'

'We're trying to save humanity, not extinguish it.'

'Bullshit. The difference between you and the BSA is so small, I don't even see it. And I'm trying real hard because the last thing I want is to be back at BSA headquarters.'

'Tell me about their headquarters.'

'I want warm clothes, clean water, and a toilet.'

'That's a lot you are asking.' He eyes me over the rim of his mug. And that's when I snap. My body explodes into motion. The chains slap in his face, shattering his mug.

But he doesn't scream for a guard. His irises flare with excitement. He kicks at my legs and barely misses as I jump aside, and round on him to yank my chains around his neck. We both believe we have the advantage over the other. He's bigger, unchained, well fed. I'm faster, and have more drive because I have very little to lose.

Before I can get a good grip on his throat, the door slams open and a guard nails me on the back of my head.

Twenty

This doesn't feel real. A soft mattress, a soft blanket. Warmth. Scents of fresh laundry and disinfectant. It's quiet here. No buzzing of half-broken light bulbs, no shouting, no slamming of doors. In the stillness, I can hear my own heart.

I whisper, 'Heartbeat,' and emptiness spreads on my tongue.

I put the loss of my word flavours aside as if they mean nothing. *Self-pity is what gets you killed,* I keep telling myself. But my heart won't listen. It yearns for Katvar. It needs to know that he's alive, that he's well and not in pain. It needs to know that he remembers who he is. And who I am.

Someone has to remember who I am because I will forget. I know that my resolve will crumble and my monster will take control. I know that as surely as I know that my wounds bleed.

I try to sit up, but a tug at my arm stops me. My wrists and ankles are shackled to the bed. Unable to hide my face in the crook of my arm, I turn my head to the wall and groan with frustration.

'Are you in pain?'

The shackles clink as I startle. I didn't know anyone was in the room with me. 'Fuck off.'

'Call if you need anything,' he says, and shuts the door.

Shuts it, doesn't slam it. That and his friendly reply are disconcerting. Where the hell did I end up? I doubt I'm far from my cell, because I can't recall a transport. Maybe I've been unconscious for days? I hate not knowing.

I rotate my joints as far as the shackles allow. My ribs hurt. My stomach, too. Dimly, I remember kicks to my abdomen. Ice Face was pretty pissed. Or excited, depending how you look at it.

My neck feels stiff, and my head hurts when I move it. Diffuse light from the ceiling stabs at my brain. Concussion is my guess. Maybe a broken rib or two.

They'll stuff me back into my box in no time.

I scan the room. It's three or four times the size of my cell and bare except for my bed and a stand with two IV bottles whose labels I can't read, then a shelf to my right and the door to my left. Next to the door is a sink with a mirror. If I can get my shackles off, I can smash the mirror and use its shards as weapons.

There's no window.

My fingers probe the shackles on my wrists. There's a small hole where a key would go. If I could get my IV out of my arm, I could use the needle to… No, wait. They probably used one of those flexible things I had at Alta's hospital. I turn my arm and stretch my neck to catch a glimpse of the material. What sticks out of my skin doesn't look like metal. Shit. Huffing, I sink back on the pillow and wonder where those flexible needle things are made and if they are expensive.

Whatever. I can't use them to pick a lock, and that's that.

My eyes scan the room again, trying to find anything nearby that's pointy or sharp. I need a lockpick and a weapon. There's a pair of scissors on the shelf, next to a few rolls of bandages, and a tray with small bottles and a syringe. All of it more than a meter out of my reach.

I squeeze my eyes shut and breathe.

A quiet knock. The door opens. A man with black skin, short curly black hair, black eyes and a white coat enters. His pants are white, too.

'You are staring,' he says. That same voice.

Of course I'm staring! I only ever *read* about people with black skin. Plus, he's the only guy aside from Ice Face who's not wearing a mask. 'Never guessed I'd meet someone with skin as ugly as mine.'

'Charming. But at least you didn't ask if I'd let you rub it.' He approaches and pulls a small squeeze light from his pocket.

'The skin or the hair?'

'Either. May I examine your pupillary reaction?'

'How's that any different from me asking you if I may rub your skin?'

'It's the difference between a physician and a racist asshole.'

'You sure you aren't both?' Do I need to point out I'd never asked to rub his skin?

He takes my retort as an invitation to examine me, and sticks his face close to mine. His nose is dented as if it had a few too many fist massages, and there's a scar running through one of his thick eyebrows. The tight black curls on his skull are pretty fascinating.

He tells me to open my eyes wide, then shines his squeeze light into them. 'How does the head feel?'

'Like a head.'

'The ribs?'

'Like ribs.'

He sighs. 'I get it. I'm one of the bad guys.'

'Yep. So when's the next cavity search coming up?'

'Aren't you being a bit prejudiced?' He turns to the shelf and fumbles with a bottle and a syringe.

'*Your* people torture me. Your people treat me worse than I would treat a dog. Your people keep me prisoner without a trial or even legal counsel.' I rattle my shackles for emphasis. 'What's in that syringe?'

'Vitamins, minerals, amino acids. You need them; you're wasting away.' He slips the needle into the tube that feeds into my arm.

'And what's in the bottles?'

'Liquids, electrolytes, glucose. I'm trying to get you physiologically stable. Have you experienced seizures?

'Nope.'

'Syncopes?'

'What?'

'Have you passed out frequently?' He draws liquid from another bottle and pumps that into my IV as well.

'Isn't that what normally happens when someone knocks you on the head?'

'Between the knocks on the head, I mean.'

'Can't remember. Maybe.'

He nods once, leans closer, and says, 'I think you've been passing out four or five times a day.'

'If there's a camera installed in my cell, you haven't been paying attention.'

He flicks his gaze to door, then back at me, and whispers so quietly I can barely understand him, 'No camera in your cell, but here. And a mic. I'll write in my report that you drifted in and out of consciousness while I was examining you, and that you've been suffering from regular syncopes for a while. Better pretend to be unresponsive now and then, and also confirm what's in my report to Colonel Johansson.'

'Who's that?'

'Your interrogator.'

Remembering the unresponsiveness, I make my body go limp and speak through my teeth, 'You mean Ice Face?'

'Huh. I guess,' he says, and turns to put the syringe away.

'Why?'

'Why what?'

I twirl my fingers at the fancy room and my IV bottles before going back to my pseudo-syncope.

His smile is bitter. 'He'll get you killed if he keeps going at you like that.'

'And a dead terrorist is of no use to you.'

'Correct.'

Well, at least I know where I stand with this guy. It would have been too nice to be seen as a human being for once. 'Are you…from Africa?' I whisper.

He claps a hand over his face and groans.

'Or was it Australia? I'm sorry, I've never listened in school, and never met a…' I trail off when he stares at me, slack-jawed. 'What?' I hiss through a corner of my mouth.

'I'm waiting for the n-word.'

What n-word? Puzzled, I squint at him. 'Like…nurse?'

His eyes grow glassy, and he doubles over wheezing with laughter.

'Fuck you, too,' I mumble. '*Don't give the terrorist any information. I get it.*'

Panting, with a palm pressed to his stomach, he's trying to pull it together. After a few deep breaths, he waves a hand at me and says, 'No, no! That's not what that was about, I just... Forget it. Ask me anything you like.'

'What's your name?' I blurt out before thinking about more strategic questions like, where the fuck I am and how I can get my hands on guns and explosives.

'I'm Dr. Johansson.'

Johansson? Really? I hike up an eyebrow. I had my first encounter with gay men years ago, but until then I had no idea that such a thing was even possible. 'You are shitting me. You and Ice Face are *married?*'

The doctor's eyes are about to bug out when he coughs like his lungs are in shreds. But he manages to croak, 'Brother. He's my brother. My parents adopted him.'

He seems to regret that last bit of information.

'Aw. Cute. I'm sure you had a splendid childhood together.'

Immediately, he switches from easy-going to stony. 'We sure did.' He checks my pulse without so much as a glance, then walks out and shuts the door.

Twenty-One

Doc told me I'm on a four-week vacation. He asked for six, but Ice Face agreed to only four, despite Doc throwing around a bunch of angry medical terms like hypokalaemia, hypophosphataemia, arrhythmia, bradycardia, syncope. I understood barely half of them when I read his report. I'm sure the other half was made up to make Ice Face feel guilty, although I doubt the man feels anything but boredom, contempt, and rage.

But for four glorious weeks, he's not going to be my problem. Which doesn't mean security has slackened. I'm fettered at all times, can't use the toilet without two guards searching it before I enter and after.

No cavity searches yet. Yay.

Yesterday, I got three warm meals (in a bowl, still warm), a shower (in a shower stall, also warm), and two twenty-minute walks through the corridor (not half as exciting as my meals and the shower). Doc says that's what I'll get every day now. They won't let me go outside, but I caught a glimpse into a lab when someone opened the door as I passed. There was a window, and behind it, barracks and tall razor wire fences, patches of melting snow on the ground, a clump of firs or spruces in the distance. Looks like a military complex in the woods, maybe smack in the rear end of Earth. Which could be in Swedish, Norwegian, Finnish or even Russian territory for all I know. On the three-day train ride, they could have taken me as far as the Black Sea. But I doubt there's snow on the ground that far south.

I keep scanning labels on bottles, shelves, books, packages of bandages and syringes and other medical supplies, canisters of chemicals, and whatever gadgets my armed and masked guards or Doc has on them, whenever I manage to catch a glimpse in passing. All of it is in English, except for a sticker on a radio a guard was carrying on his hip. It was in Cyrillic.

In other words: I don't have the slightest where I am.

ICE FACE walks into my room without knocking. Aw, shit. And here I was, thinking he was going to give me a break. He doesn't even smirk. Just looks like he owns the place, and me.

He probably does.

'No guards?' I ask.

He twitches a shoulder. 'It's more fun without them, isn't it?'

I sit up in my bed as far as the chains allow. Which isn't far. My bladder begs for a toilet break. What shit timing.

He pulls up a chair and sits. Crosses his arms over his chest as he leans back. He shuts his eyes and murmurs, 'I suggest you talk. I'm the good guy here.'

A mad giggle rolls up my chest. 'Really?'

A corner of his mouth tweaks a little. He's such an arse biscuit. He zeroes his gaze in on me as someone knocks on the door.

'Enter,' he says.

Three people stride into the room. Two men in combat boots and pants that look brand new and completely untouched by combat of any sort. And a woman in a skirt, of all things. She even holds a notepad and pen in her hands. Her eyes ogle me over silver-rimmed glasses.

The guys I can deal with, but she throws me off. She's artificial in every way.

'Mickaela Capra, you are accused of treason,' she says to her notepad, not me.

The men keep their gazes trained on a point above my head.

The woman doesn't wait for my reply. She draws a quick squiggle on her notepad, and rattles on, 'You are working for Erik Vandemeer — your father and head of the BSA. Together, you laid a trap for your team and the troops that came to your aid. None of them made it out alive. Furthermore, you helped the BSA cause the meltdown of a nuclear power plant, leading to massive radioactive contamination of South Taiwan. You, Vandemeer, and two of his men subsequently fled that island. In the ensuing two years, you helped destroy several Sequencer bases, and got hundreds of our people killed.' Here, she finally looks up. 'And you destroyed our global satellite network. Our greatest asset. Our means of reconnaissance and communication. Gone in the blink of an eye.'

'Maura,' one of the guys presses through his teeth.

Does he think she gave away some tidbit of secret intel? You'd have to be a complete douchewaffle to *not* know that Earth's satellite network was a great asset.

She cuts him an annoyed glance, which tells me they are definitely *not* BSA, no matter how they treat me. Because if they were, Maura would not be saying a peep without a male telling her to, would never dare show a male disrespect, because they'd mop the floor with her if she so much as tried to roll her eyes at them.

I should be relieved, but I'm not. Sequencers are supposed to be fighting the BSA, not torturing ex-prisoners of the Bull Shit Army. Thoroughly pissed by this circus, I say, 'Twelve days.'

'Excuse me?'

'Not *in the blink of an eye*. It took seventeen satellites equipped with particle-beam guns and nine swarms of autonomous parasitic nanosatellites two hundred ninety-four hours to destroy more than five thousand satellites. It took *twelve days*, not *the blink of an eye*.'

She stares at me. 'Is that all you have to say?'

'I'd like to know if you guys always take torture lessons from the BSA, or if Ice Face is the only intern you sent to them.'

Her perfect eyebrows form two crooked lines. 'In times of war, our methods are justified. We serve the greater good.'

'And at which point is the price for the greater good too high?'

'There is no price too high,' she says primly.

I want to slap her stupid glasses off her face and paint her trimmed eyebrows with a fat charcoal stick. It's child-ish, but who cares. 'If that's true, the world will be full of assholes once you and the BSA are done with it.'

She pushes her glasses up her nose, glances down at

her notepad, and says, 'We have footage of you and another person killing five of our men on Svalbard. You dragged one of them into their solar plane, and took off with it. What did you do with him? Is he alive?'

'They attacked us without reason. Your footage shows that, yes?' I wait in vain for an answer.

'What happened to the man you took?'

'I fed him to the dogs.' I'm not going to mention that most of the guy was eaten by me and Katvar.

'Barbaric!' one of the men spits. Both are blunt-jawed and clean shaven. Both have Scandinavian looks. Bright blue eyes, pale hair. Muscular prime examples of the species. The BSA would love them.

I wonder why none of them wear masks.

Maura clears her throat with a high-pitched cough. 'You asked for legal counsel. I'm more than happy to offer my skills to you. Your trial will be in two months. Until then, you'd do well to tell us everything.'

'I can tell you only what I know.'

'Of course.' She gifts me a smile, and gestures at the edge of the bed I'm strapped to. 'May I sit?'

I narrow my eyes at her. 'Be my guest.'

The two guys she came in with are keeping their muzzles ready as she parks one butt cheek on the mattress and on a chain that's holding my ankle to the frame.

'Can you move your bum from my ankle chain, please? It kinda hurts.'

Again that prim little smile. She doesn't move a millimetre. 'Now, Mickaela, tell me why the BSA are invading Norwegian territory.'

'How is that related to my case?'

'It shows goodwill on your part to share everything we need to know in order to stop them.'

Exhaling slowly, I shut my eyes and count to three. Legal counsel my arse. 'I need to use the toilet.'

Maura doesn't give a shit. 'Why did they attack Tromsø?'

'I don't know.'

'What was their goal on Taiwan? Why take Taiwan and then make its south uninhabitable?'

'I'm not sure. Runner and I had our theories. Taiwan had a satellite control centre, which seems to have been the BSA's primary target. They took it and then rigged the front and back doors.'

'They were expecting you?'

'Wouldn't you?'

'Answer the question,' Ice Face says.

'Huh? Didn't I just point out that it would be idiotic not to expect the enemy when invading their territory? Do you think the BSA are all lobotomised?'

Maura taps her pencil against the edge of her notepad. 'What was your role for the BSA before and during the Taiwan incident?'

'I need to use the toilet.'

'Not before you've answered my question.'

'I'm going to piss my pants if you don't let me use the toilet.'

She spreads a hand on her thigh and shakes her head. 'I'm *really* sorry, but I can't let you go before you've answered my question.'

'I didn't work for the BSA before, during, or after Taiwan. Can I use the toilet now?'

'You are lying. You are the daughter of the commander.'

'And you think that means anything to him?'

'He saved your life in Taiwan,' Ice Face says.

I swivel my head to him. The dull glimmer in his eyes

122

gives me the creeps. 'Erik led me and my friends into a trap. He wanted me, yes. He tried to pull me onto his side, to make me some kind of girl mascot. He wanted me to draw more women to the BSA.'

'As I said. He saved your life. You enjoyed special treatment at the hands of the BSA. No one ever comes out alive and unscathed.'

'Unscathed? *Unscathed?*' My throat works hard to spit out air.

Maura leans closer to me. 'You know what I believe? I believe Erik Vandermeer taught you everything he knows, and then he sent you to Svalbard to destroy our satellite network.'

'Are you nuts? *You* ignored all the evidence that showed the BSA hacked your satellite network. We sent you that information long before we engaged in battle on Taiwan! Fuck, Erik was a *Sequencer*, a satellite communications specialist. He knew how to access your toys. He didn't need anyone to do it for him. Kat and Runner warned you. Ben warned you. And what did *you* do? You ignored them. And then you let Runner die in Taiwan! You abandoned him. Your best strategist and sharpshooter! You let *everyone* die! Because of you, I wasted away for two years at BSA headquarters. I was raped, tortured, and my...' Hearing my shrill voice bouncing off the walls, I shut my mouth. I'm not telling these people about my dead daughter. She's in my heart. They won't get her.

'Your what?'

'Fuck. Off.'

Maura straightens her skirt. 'I am done here. She's all yours.' She clips her pen to her notepad and stalks out of the room with cheerful *click-clicks* of her dainty heels.

Ice Face stands and taps his knuckles against the metal

rails of my bed. 'What did you do during your two years at BSA headquarters?'

'I did what I was told.'

'An obedient daughter.'

'A prisoners with the will to survive.' Which is a lie. I didn't want to live in that hell. But I wanted to take Erik down with me, even knowing that my chances for success were very limited. Nonexistent, in hindsight.

'A *prisoner*.' His tone is mocking.

'If you take a closer look, you'll notice that I am a woman. What do you think the BSA does to women?'

I scan the other two men who seem to be waiting for something. 'What, you forgot your flail? Or was it razors. A hammer?' I ask.

One of them pulls a small black case from his back pocket, and snaps it open. A glint of a needle makes my skin crawl.

'Two hours for now?' he asks Ice Face.

Ice Face stuffs his hands in his trouser pockets and sucks air through his teeth. 'Whatever you want. I promised my brother I wouldn't touch her for four weeks.'

'What's…this?' I croak, my gaze stuck to the syringe.

'Paralysis and pain. So that next time you'll be more cooperative.'

'I am!' I try to wiggle away from them, but my chains hold. One guy sits on my arm, the other jabs the needle into a vein.

A minute or two later my tongue feels swollen and furry, my teeth and feet as if they don't exist at all. I try to say, 'Did I tell you that I have only eight toes?' for no reason whatsoever, but only 'duh-huh-huh' comes out.

Pain begins to stab my body. Everywhere.

And I'm almost grateful because it makes me forget the wound Katvar's absence strikes into my chest.

Twenty-Two

I read somewhere that time is not a line stretching from past to future, but that it's a structure comparable to a crystalline sponge. The dude who came up with that theory — and I'm pretty sure it was a dude — must have had a happy life with nothing to worry about. He probably never even did the dishes. He claimed there's no "now." I agree with that bit. There *is* no "now." There is only before and after.

This is after.

I'm not sure when my so-called vacation stopped and the normal terrorist treatment resumed. I'm still in a hospital room, strapped to a bed. I'm still fed three times a day, walked twice a day.

But everything else has changed. They use every one of my needs to cause discomfort. When I need to use the toilet, they rush me to the bathroom at breakneck speed, then rush me back out thirty seconds later. Or they lock me into the bathroom for two hours, shackled to a rail on the wall.

They postpone feeding time until my stomach roars, then serve a double portion and insist I finish it in three minutes. Or they give me a bucket of watery soup and wait until my bladder is about to burst. Then they wait two hours longer before allowing me to relieve myself.

I sleep lightly, always on edge. Several times each night, someone rushes into my room and shouts at me, then checks my shackles and leaves, or drags me to an interrogation room just to shackle me to a chair and leave me until morning. Or I'm dragged to a bathroom because I am to fucking pee when someone tells me to pee, not when I need to.

They only ever leave me alone after they've injected me.

At first, there's only numbness. I don't feel my body at all for the first minute or two. Those are the best moments of my day. I imagine Katvar floating next to me, holding my hand. And then I'm breathing needles. The pain enters through my mouth, spreads through my lungs, and creeps into every limb.

My jailers don't even need to work up a sweat. The drug — whatever it is — does their work for them. They stubbornly keep giving it to me every day right after I stubbornly keep telling them what they don't want to hear: the truth.

It's not because I hope they'll believe me one day.

It's part of my escape plan.

Whoever administers the drug — usually Ice Face or Doc — waits a few minutes, and hooks me up to a machine that says *beeb* with every contraction of my heart.

126

Then an arm and a leg are unshackled, and I'm rolled onto my side so I don't suffocate in my own vomit. The puking is a side effect of the drug and the paralysis. It doesn't bother me. I don't really feel it when it happens. I'm busy with the agony that's crawling through the marrow of my bones. I'm trying to *scream*, but I can only produce tired huffs. At the most.

The needle sliding into my arm is my reference point. That's when I start counting. Somewhere between seven thousand and seven thousand five hundred, the sharp pain flattens to a dull throb and the itching begins. It makes me want to claw the skin off my bones.

They give me the same dose every day. I keep an eye on the liquid in the syringe. And I am waiting for the day my count drops to below seven thousand because I heard Doc tell Ice Face that my body might get used to the drug.

Of course, Ice Face is arrogant and cruel enough to keep giving me a daily shot anyway. He doesn't seem to believe his brother. He doesn't believe me either. Or anyone, probably.

And so I wait for my body to adjust and learn to inactivate the drug.

And then I'll use the needle Doc forgot to take with him a few days ago. Or maybe it's been weeks.

Crystallised sponge my ass. Time is congealed dog vomit.

I'VE DEVELOPED an unhealthy fear of scissors.

When Ice Face interrogates me, he clips his nails. Every fucking day. There's really nothing left to clip, but he manages to shave the thinnest slivers of nail, callus and hangnail off his fingertips. I catch myself waiting for him to draw blood. It's like a compulsion. I *need* to see blood. Because that's what my heart beats. *Blood*. I'm thirsty for it. I want to bleed Ice Face dry and rip the fucking nails off his fingers.

He's watching me now. He's lingering in my room longer and longer after giving me the injection. At first, I was afraid that he knew I was waiting for the drug to wear off. I had nightmares about him sneaking up at me after I'd finally managed to move my limbs enough to pick the lock of my shackles.

But he really just waits for the others to leave us alone. Then he waits a little longer, relishing those moments I can't talk back to him. And then the creep clips *my* fingernails. He's gentle about it, but there's always that touch of insanity in his gaze.

Now he comes over to sit on my bed. I shift my eyes in their sockets as he picks up my right hand. It's the one he unshackled earlier. It might seem like no big thing. A man touching a woman to clip her nails. But he and I know that he can cut me deep, and I can't even scream. He and I know that I am at his mercy every minute of every day and every night, and that his holding the tips of my paralysed fingers between two sharp blades drives that point home like nothing else can.

He watches how fury, despair, and pain roar through me. He knows I feel exposed and vulnerable. There's nothing between my flesh and his. And he loves this. He loves that I am put in my place, and that he's the one doing it.

I'M at six thousand four hundred when the pain lessens. I

can't believe it! How long has it been? Three weeks? Three months?

It's hard to not move a muscle, hard to remain limp and let everyone believe their drug is working just fine. I don't know if anyone is watching. Doc said there's a mic and a camera installed in this room. Might have been a lie. Or maybe not.

I keep counting to seven thousand five hundred and then start to move.

TODAY I FIGURED out what R&D means. I've been wondering since I spotted those letters sewn on the lapel of a lab coat that hung by one of the many grey doors lining the corridor. R&D means Research and Development. I try to fit this with the many small things I've observed since I was brought here. There's a lab on this level. Judging from rare noises above and below my room, this building has several levels. The ones just above and below are probably not part of the hospital. If this even *is* a hospital, which I doubt by now. Especially because of the research and development part.

The level I'm on is quiet. Footfalls, and doors opening and closing. Calm conversations of which I catch bits and pieces. I can't make sense of most of it, so I ask Doc when he walks into my room. 'What's vayhotherapy?'

He nearly drops his key ring before stuffing it into his pocket. 'I'm not allowed to say.' He flicks a nervous glance at the door.

'How long have I been here?'

He shakes his head.

'Is it spring?'

'I'm not allowed to tell you that.'

'Are the snowdrops blooming?' I try again.

He shuts his eyes. 'I'm not allowed—'

'Is the sun shining? Are bumblebees flying? Can you hear birds sing? Do you feel the fucking wind on your face? Do you? Because *I do not!*' I yank on my shackles. 'Fuck you and your brother. Fuck everyone in this compound. Humanity doesn't want to be saved by people like you.'

'You are in no position to say that. In no position.' He fluffs his plumage like an overzealous rooster.

'And who put *you* in that position?'

'I have seen things that—'

'Oh, shut up already! *You* have seen things? Have you seen the BSA burn women alive and gang-rape children? Have *you* been tortured by the BSA *and* the Sequencers? Have you?'

'Our species would be lost if not for us.' Inside his pockets, he fists the fabric of his coat. His keys are clinking.

'Funny. The BSA say the same thing. Why can't either of you just let people live the way they want to live? Or actually *help* them for a change? You have all these grand plans for saving humanity, but do you actually know what the term "hospital" means in the real world?'

'I am aware of the state of healthcare. Or lack thereof. We cannot afford to ship all our medical supplies to people. There wouldn't be anything left. We need all our resources to study the current pandemics and develop cures.'

'Is that what vayotherapy is for?'

He hesitates a moment, then nods once, and whispers, 'It's called virotherapy.'

'Ugh. How noble of you,' I grunt. 'But there's a big fat hole in your excuse.'

'It's *not* an excuse!'

'It is. If you can't afford to ship your medical supplies

to people now, what makes you think you'll be able to later?'

He snorts. 'I've been working on this my whole life. We have been working on this. And we'll finish it.'

'So you *and* your buddies have been lying to yourselves your entire lives. Smart.'

'I… I'm not talking to you anymore.'

'Does that mean I can go home now?'

He slams the door. It's about time I touched a nerve.

———

Three thousand one hundred. The itching is driving me nuts, but the pain is gone. Keeping my face in what I hope is a passive mask, I contract my thighs to see how much muscle control I've got. They do what my brain is telling them. My right arm is curled over my left, and my left hand is hidden under the blanket. I move my fingers. Thumb, index finger, middle and ring finger. Pinkie. They are a bit clumsy. Not yet ready to pick a lock.

———

I hate talking with Ice Face. He's such a bleeding fuck-tangle, I'm tempted to tell him the lies he wants to hear. "Yes, I'm the BSA's second in command and we're planning for world domination. This, this, and this is how we'll go about it. You win, I lose."

Gah.

But when I say, 'I don't think the BSA have anything to match your bioweapons,' I hit gold.

Ice Face's facade freezes over. I didn't know that was possible.

He even goes so far as to confirm my suspicion verbally.

'If the BSA knows about our arsenal of biological weapons, how come they didn't prepare for them? Why hasn't this compound ever been attacked?' Smiling mildly, he shakes his head as though he's disappointed his kid dirtied her knees. 'Lies, lies, and more lies. Your value to us is getting…shall I say, questionable? I thought better of you. Alas…' He lets the words hang in the space between us. That's how he works. He wants my mind to fill in the blanks for him. Just as he lets the drug deliver pain for him, and lets his brother fix me up whenever he goes overboard with his methods.

'We continue tomorrow.' As he leaves the interrogation room, I know that this will be another night spent shackled to a metal chair.

Two thousand eight hundred. It's now or never. Doc has pulled the blanket up to my chin because I was cold this morning and couldn't stop shaking. My hands are hidden from the camera, but I still hope no one is watching. Millimetre by millimetre, I slip my right hand under the mattress and pull on the needle I've hidden deep in a fold, then carefully bend its pointy end. I slip it into the keyhole of the shackle and begin to probe for something that gives under pressure.

My hands tremble and my fingertips feel numb, but I'm pretty sure nothing inside this shit handcuff is moving. I keep counting the time, and at three thousand five hundred my heart races so fast I get lightheaded. My palms are slick with sweat and I have to keep wiping them on the sheets. Why the hell is this not working?

Taking a deep breath, I try to calm myself and think about an alternative. My mind picks apart the locking mechanism of my shackles — or rather, what I believe the locking mechanism should be. I was able to pick the shackles Erik put on me in the Vault. But that was two years ago, and I haven't had time to practice.

Four thousand five hundred.

I'm fucked.

I'm so fu—

Wait a second.

I remove the bent needle from the lock, straighten it as best I can, and slip it between the ratchet teeth and the ratchet itself. And then I press down on it, pinching my wrist hard until I feel how the rasp of teeth against the ratchet smooths away.

Gingerly, I pull at the cuff.

My wrist comes free.

Part Three

No one starts a war—or rather, no one in his sense ought to do so—without first being clear in his mind what he intends to achieve by that war and how he intends to conduct it.

Carl Von Clausewitz

Twenty-Three

I kick the blanket off with my free foot and get to work on the remaining ankle cuff. Time is racing away from me. Once more, I jam the needle between ratchet teeth and ratchet, but I can see already that the cuff is on too tight. There's not enough space to push down to open it. Twisting my leg and rotating the cuff, I try to find a better position. I press down hard on the needle and the cuff. The metal cuts into my skin, but the pain barely registers. I have to get the fuck out of here, even if it costs me my foot.

My time in the hands of the BSA taught me that the worst thing you can do when someone takes you prisoner is to think they have absolute control and you are powerless. If you believe that, you won't be able to tackle your problems. There are always options and possibilities. Even if you are trapped in a concrete box, denied a toilet, a bed, clothes, food and clean water. Your options aren't comparable to the luxuries you are used to, so you suffer. But when you learn to use what's given to you, you find a way to manage. You have choices, even if each and every small choice comes with a heavy price.

But amputating my foot isn't one of them. I need both feet to run, and there's no knife within my reach anyway. The cuff is now so tight, it cuts off my circulation. The shit thing just won't open. Panting, I scan the room.

That's when I hear footfalls in the hallway. Someone approaching in a run. My throat closes in panic. I lunge to the IV stand, and nearly fall over and face plant the floor as the shackle jerks me back. I stretch until my spine hurts. My fingertips brush my target. Just as the door bursts open, I manage to grab the stand and whirl around, only somewhat assured by the cold, hard metal in my hands.

Doc stands in the frame, black knuckles paling against the door handle. He scans the IV stand in my grip, my face, and says in a voice as cold as his brother's, 'Your friends are attacking.'

For a fraction of a second, I grin and my hope soars, but then I realise that he and I have a disagreement about who my friends really are. My knees feel like water. 'I need a gun.'

He snorts. 'I'm not an idiot.'

I clench my jaw. 'I keep telling you the Bull Shit Army is my enemy. Give me a gun and I'll help you.' Slowly, I lower the IV stand to show him I mean no harm. I must look pathetic. Rumpled clothes and hair, balancing on one leg, the other stretched over the bed and shackled to the frame. And I'm wielding an IV stand, of all things. 'Please. A gun. And a key.' I thrust my chin at the shackle.

There might be doubt in his eyes. Or maybe not. But for a brief moment, he considers my request. I don't dare breathe.

He drags his gaze away from me, steps back, and leaves.

I roar my fury at the shut door.

It just can't be. Of all the days the BSA could have attacked this specific base, they pick the very minute I'm trying to escape. My reality is worse than my nightmares. Every step I take, my legs are kicked from under me. I feel like I'm drowning in glue.

Bellowing, I yank at the chain that holds me, knowing full well that all I'll accomplish is to bloody my ankle.

'*Think*, Micka,' I groan through my teeth. Is there nothing I can use? Really nothing? My roving gaze stops on the IV stand. It's made of metal. Just like my chains. Just like the frame of my bed.

I slam the stand against the bed frame over and over, pausing only briefly to listen to the growing noise in the corridor. People are evacuating the building. Someone shouts a command. They all pass my door, ignoring the loud crashes I produce.

Looks like I'm not important right now. A good time to get lost.

One leg of the IV stand is about to come off and I haven't even put a dent in the bed frame or the chain. My ankle is bleeding from two cuts, making me hot with fury and despair. Bellowing, I smack the chain. Two legs spring off the IV stand, which is now bent. And not a scratch to the chain.

Part of me wants to keep bashing in things. The other part knows I have to find an alternative because *this* isn't working. I pick up one of the broken-off legs. Its foot is made of rubber, its base is narrow and pretty sharp where it was welded to the stand. I flip it in my hand and consider my shackled ankle.

The sharp end of the leg slips easily between the double strands of the cuff. Bracing my foot against the bed frame, I twist my makeshift lever in the shackle. The shackle's edge cuts into my shin. I keep pushing until I could swear there's a crunch of metal grinding over bone. I increase the pressure. It's my only option. Other than cutting off my foot.

The metal gives without the faintest noise. Might be I didn't hear the screech because of my own shout of pain.

I peel the shackle off my ankle, and smooth a ragged flap of skin back over my flesh. Fuck, my leg hurts. I need to stabilise my ankle and stop the bleeding before I leave here.

I hobble over to the shelf where Doc keeps a few supplies, and pick up bandages and disinfectant. My butt hits the floor harder than I planned. My fingers are trembling with pain and fear of failure as I clean the wound and wrap a bandage around it. I grab another roll and pad to the mirror by the door, smash it in and pick up a large shard. I wrap the bandage around its base, letting only the pointy end stick out. Then I grab the IV stand, break off the remaining leg, and…realise I'm barefoot.

The snow outside might not be a problem in the first hour or two, but I can't afford freezing more of my toes off. I have only eight left. And this being a battleground now, sharp things are probably littering the floors.

Quickly, I use the shard to slice and rip my bed sheet into strips, wrap my feet in several layers of them, and make sure they work like shoes and not like tripwires.

Then, I step to the door, press my ear to it and listen.

There's nothing. No running, no shouting. Looks like the Sequencers have fled. I have only moments until the BSA show up here.

Sucking in two deep breaths, I press down on the door handle.

Twenty-Four

The place looks abandoned, but other than that, unchanged. I whisper along the corridor and slip through one of its many grey doors in search of a window. I need to see what's going on; I can't just run blindly at the enemy. Especially since *both* sides are the enemy. It doesn't matter how glorious they think they are, or that they believe the world will soon be saved, thanks to them. Their intentions really don't matter. What they are willing to do and what they refuse to do are what matters. And at that, the Sequencers have turned out to be a lot like the BSA.

I find what I'm looking for as I enter a lab. Work-benches, some looking like desks, others like see-through boxes, line the walls. Small plates with hundreds of tiny indentations are stacked inside the see-through boxes. A forgotten burner sputters a yellow flame. Several monitors show reports and calculations, and there are schematics that look like bushes or trees, but with species names and numbers instead of leaves.

Ducking, I approach a window and scan outside. There's a courtyard with a pond that has a fountain at its centre and is belted by tall reeds and greenery that blooms purple and yellow. There's even a pink pond lily. It must be...July? August? That can't be true. Didn't I spot melting snow only...a few weeks ago?

I push the thought aside. What really matters to me now is access to weapons. My eyes search the room. There's something that looks a bit like a gun, but with a small cartridge for gas instead of...

Uh oh, did someone leave a flamethrower for the evil terrorist?

I push down the trigger. After two sharp clicks, a blue flame shoots out of the muzzle. The flame is only as long as my hand but better than nothing. I make to pocket the small flamethrower, but realise halfway that I don't have any pockets. Only a pair of slacks and a shirt, both without pockets because a prisoner doesn't need that crap, does she?

Scanning for clothes and more weapons, I run through connecting doors from one lab to the next, ducking whenever I come across a window — all of which face the empty courtyard.

A few moments later, I'm one ridiculous wool cardigan with a reindeer motif (but with two pockets!), two flamethrowers, a large pair of scissors, and several scalpels richer. I find a toolbox under a workbench, and inside is the solution to most of my problems: lots of zip ties.

There's also a humongous pipe wrench. What do researchers need pipe wrenches, flamethrowers, and zip ties for?

I abandon my mirror shard, and use the wrench and a pair of pliers to break off one half of the scissors. Then I zip tie it to the bottom of the IV stand. A spear is a far cry from a high-precision rifle, but better than nothing.

I button the cardigan, heft my makeshift spear, and exit the lab section to try the doors on the other side of the hallway.

All are locked.

Knowing that I've already been on this level way too long, I press my ear to the exit, twist the knob, and step into a stairwell.

A light bulb jitters above me. I lean my back against the door, and prick my ears for footfalls, voices, or anything that would tell me about enemy movement. It's strangely quiet here. More like a cemetery than a battleground.

Where *is* everybody?

I inch forward and peek over the bannister. A guy in black two levels down is pointing his muzzle in my direction. I jerk back as a shot is fired. The report echoes through the emptiness. He mutters into a radio and receives a scratchy response.

Gazing at my small flamethrowers and my scissor IV stand, I try to convince myself that I'm not pathetic at all and that I'm not going to die in a reindeer cardigan.

Hurried movements on the lower levels send my heart into my throat. I can't return to the lab wing, and I can't stay here or run down. Hoping that upstairs isn't just another dead end, I open the door behind me and let it fall shut, trying to make the Bull Shit Army believe I went that way.

Then I slink up the stairs.

One level up, I find a locked door. I don't dare try my spear on it, because that would give me away. The next level is locked, too. I race up another set of stairs and find one door. I try the knob.

It won't budge.

That's it, then. No cover, and the only way out is right into the raised guns of the BSA. Sounds of boots on concrete and metal are coming closer.

I catch myself muttering, 'I'm not going back. I'm not going back.'

Sinking my teeth into the inside of my cheeks, I shut myself up.

I hear them splitting up on the level I came from. Boots shuffle. A door snaps shut. Someone climbs the stairs.

One guy. Just one. I can deal with one guy.

But I need more space to move. My feet carry me down one flight. I press my back into the darkest corner, slip the flamethrowers in my waistband at the small of my back, and park the spear against the wall behind me.

My pulse thuds in my ears. *I am not going back.* Not to the Sequencers and definitely not to the BSA. Even if I break my vow to Katvar, I will not be a prisoner again. I curl and uncurl my fingers, calm my breathing, focus.

A bearded man in black combat gear rounds the corner. The moment he spots me, his pistol swivels to my centre mass. He seems quick enough. A bit bulky, though.

I lift my hands in surrender, plastering a nervous smile on my face.

He doesn't see that even though my hands are empty, I'm not harmless. All he sees is an exhausted, scared girl in a ridiculous cardigan, with strips of white fabric around her feet instead of boots.

Grinning, he relaxes his stance, and reaches for the radio on his hip.

Big. Fucking. Mistake.

I rotate my body away from the line of fire as I lunge

for the gun, and jerk it up, aside, and out of his hand in less than half a second. At the same time, my injured foot hits his ballsack. He goes down with a squeak. I smack the butt of his gun against his temple to make sure he stays down. With a painful huff, he folds in on himself. His radio clatters to the floor, skids through the bannister, and tumbles, tumbles, tumbles, announcing to everyone and their fleas that a BSA soldier just went down. And sure enough, lots of noise is coming from below now. Clattering, loud voices, and someone chewing on his radio.

At least I have a gun.

As the guy by my feet moves again, I whack him on the head for good, then frisk his limp body. Two pistols, four fresh clips, and a knife. I feel much better already.

'Oy, scrotum mullets!' I shout. 'I've got your comrade. If you don't want me to hang him by his testicles from the bannister, I'd suggest you clear the building.' I make my voice croaky and low. The last thing I need is anyone from the Bull Shit Army recognising me and reporting me to Erik.

A few moments of silence are followed by some more chewing on the radio. They seem to be waiting for shit to trickle back down the chain of command. Someone starts a heated argument. I hope they kill each other in a brawl. What a bunch of amateurs. Definitely not from Headquarters, and I'm glad for that.

They won't know who I am.

The breath of relief freezes in my mouth as someone from below shouts, 'Is your name Mickaela Capra?'

Twenty-Five

'Fuck,' I mutter under my breath.

'Don't shoot!' the guy shouts. 'We're not here to harm you.'

Sure. You're not here to kill me. Just to drag me back to hell, marry me to some sadistic pig, and force me to kill innocent people for you.

The man I knocked out starts moving again. Quickly, I check the chambers of both pistols, and find a round in each. I'm not sure if his guns are any good, or if they'll jam or even blow up in my hand the moment I squeeze the trigger. I decide to test them before I try to shoot myself out of here.

Besides, the Bull Shit Army needs a reminder of who they're dealing with.

I aim at the prone man who's just regaining consciousness and put a bullet in his head and one in his chest. One BSA asshat down, an unknown number of asshats to go.

They start shouting in earnest now.

I'm ready to dance.

I place one gun on the floor, and use my free hand to pull a flamethrower from my waistband, then risk a quick peek over the bannister. They are coming up fast, careful to stay out of sight. 'Stop shooting!' someone shouts over and over.

Idiots.

I drop the first flamethrower down the stairwell and fire my pistol at its gas cartridge.

A fireball erupts with an ear-splitting *WOOOMP!* and I have barely enough time to jerk back before flames can singe off my eyebrows.

Cries of pain bounce off bare concrete walls.

'Got your ballsacks singed?' I call down.

'You fucking bitch! We came to get you out of here!'

I bark a laugh. 'I'd rather die than go back to you, you butt maggots! Piss off or I'll bomb you to fucking hell! One... Two...' I don't wait for "three." I drop the last flamethrower. My index finger curls against the trigger when I hear a hoarse cry of, 'Micka noooo!'

That...voice...

I'm dying inside.

My mouth opens to shout a warning as a round spins out of the barrel. Whatever I wanted to say drowns in the explosion. Nothing but survival instinct forces my body to duck away from the heat. My eyes are shut. I can't get them to open.

That voice.

I suck in a breath and scream, 'Katvar?'

'Micka?' he croaks.

Oh no! Nononono. 'Not you. Not *you!*' I can't feel my body, or anything, really. Only the hard metal of a gun in each hand. Despair steals my breath. Katvar taken by the BSA is a hundred times worse than *anything* they have done to me.

'He signs that he's okay,' a man shouts from further down. 'He wants me to tell you to stop shooting. You singed off Kioshi's beard, and he's really mad.'

'I'll kill this bitch!' another man bellows. 'She's killed Lars and Vi—' He's shut up by what sounds like a punch to his mouth.

The other man cuts in, 'You heard him. If you so much as put a finger on your guns or explosives, we'll make sure you won't leave this building in one piece.'

'Kioshi? Katvar?' Terror is making my voice squeaky as rubber. I don't give a shit about the threats to my life. Katvar's life though… That's a whole different world of pain.

'Girl, you have a serious trigger-finger problem. Can I send Katvar up without getting him killed?'

That's Kioshi's voice. *Really* Kioshi's voice! 'Why are you with the BSA?'

A man groans. Another mutters something, and someone else shouts, 'Hurry the fuck up, will ya?'

'Katvar will explain. *Don't shoot!*' Kioshi shouts.

My entire frame trembles like grass in the wind. 'If you guys are fucking with me, I'll bring down this building.'

'We get it! You made your point, girl. Now, can we speed up this shit? People are hurt and dying.'

'Get them to the hospital wing,' I say.

'What hospital wing? There is no hospital wing.'

'The lab wing you just searched. There's a room with a bed and medical supplies.'

They begin to move, and I can hear that I must have

149

caused a lot of damage. Muffled cries of pain. Feet dragging heavily. Groans. And in the noise, a pair of boots steadily climbing toward me.

I scoot back into a corner and prop both wrists on my knees, aiming through the bannister to where the head of the approaching guy will show up. My pulse jumps. Blood is thundering in my ears.

When a man comes into view, I wilt. The hair along the top of his head is braided tightly against his skull. The side of his head is shorn, and a jagged pink scar cuts through the stubble. My view swims when his eyes lock on mine. He's alive! He's alive and…dressed all in black. No bow, no quiver. The pistol looks foreign on his hip. I barely find the energy to keep my head up and breathe.

A wail slips through my teeth.

As Katvar covers the short distance, my quivering hands press one muzzle against the soft flesh beneath my jaw and point the other at his heart. 'I'm not going back to them. And you aren't either!'

Colour drains from his face. He sinks to his knees in front of me, and whispers in his cruelly damaged voice, 'My love.'

I can't produce anything but a sob.

Carefully, he peels the guns from my grip. I collapse against him. Claw his back and pull him close, never wanting to let go. I keen pain, shock, and relief against the skin of his throat. And then I pull back to shake him. 'Why? Why the BSA? Did they take Alta? How did you… Are you hurt? Did I hurt you?'

He shakes his head wildly. 'And You? Are you hurt? Did the Sequencers treat you well?'

'I'm fine.'

He catches the lie but says nothing, wraps his fingers

around my wrists, and pulls my hand to his mouth to kiss my knuckles. 'Your absence hurt,' he signs with one hand, then places my palm above his heart.

I clench my teeth. 'Why are you with the fucking BSA?'

Twenty-Six

'We need to get a move on!' someone shouts from below.

Katvar sets his chin and nods toward the staircase. 'I'll explain on the way—'

I grab the front of his shirt. 'The hell you will! You tell me *now* what you and Kioshi are doing here, and why... Why the Bull Shit Army?'

He pulls me to my feet, and signs, 'They aren't BSA. They are people from Alta. They pretend to be the BSA when they raid a Sequencer base, and pretend to be Sequencers when they rob the BSA.'

My jaw goes slack. 'They do that often?'

He lifts a shoulder and nods. Like it's totally normal to fuck with the two most powerful organisations in modern history.

'And Kioshi? What's *he* doing here?'

'Later. I promise. First, we have to help move supplies.'

I follow him to the level I just escaped. The stink of burnt fabric, hair and skin is overwhelming. We pass the bodies of two men. Their exposed skin is marbled black and scarlet. Ribbons of congealed blood trail from noses, ears, and mouth.

Katvar's lips compress at the sight, but he says nothing.

We reach the entrance and my legs grow heavy. Crossing the threshold into the corridor takes all my courage. I'm drained.

Katvar explains that this group is assigned to filch medical supplies, while another group is responsible for weapons and ammo. We search this level, with my room the obvious place to start, but all of the few available things are already being used on the men I injured. Among them, Kioshi. One side of his beard is singed, the skin above it, red. A missing eyebrow gives him a half-surprised, half-snarky look.

He catches my petrified expression and grins. 'My hat took the brunt of it. Poor thing, that.' He points at a black puddle of fabric on the floor. A ribbon of smoke curls up from it.

'I'm sorry,' I say, not sure if I should extend my apologies to everyone in the room. 'I didn't know.'

A man on my bed grunts. He, too, has blood leaking from his ears and nose. His legs tremble as someone picks at the remnants of his sleeve to clean a horribly burnt arm. Without looking up, the man tending to the wound asks, 'Is that a painkiller in the unlabelled bottle behind me?'

'No. It's the opposite.'

He pauses. 'And what's that supposed to mean?'

'They use it for torture.'

Katvar stops breathing. I sense him taking in the room

with fresh eyes: the shackles dangling from the bed frame; the drug; the lack of a window; the broken mirror.

The man continues his work of picking burnt fabric from the other's wound, peeling off dead skin glued to each piece of cloth. 'We'll need a stretcher for him.' At the request, someone leaves.

This whole scenario feels surreal. Katvar, Kioshi, and a bunch of strangers crowding the room where I was kept and tortured for weeks. Only minutes ago, I thought I'd rather die than come back in here.

I clear my throat and turn to Kioshi. 'How are Saida and Gnat? And the little ones?'

His gaze empties. Katvar nudges me with his elbow, and signs, 'The BSA retaliated.'

'No!' My fist presses into the hollow of my stomach. Although I knew better, a part of me had hoped the Lume were too small a tribe to be considered important by the BSA. It was Katvar's clan that nursed me back to health and helped me cross five thousand kilometres of snow and ice to reach Svalbard and blow up all the satellites. They gave me so much, and paid with their lives.

'How many?'

'Too many,' Kioshi answers. 'There's not a man, woman or child who hasn't lost a family member.

I reach out and place my hand on his shoulder. 'I'm sorry.'

He covers my hand with his own and gives a gentle squeeze. 'You did well. Both of you. Birket would have been proud.'

'Birket is dead?' I whisper.

Kioshi nods.

'Did Sari make it?'

'She did. Sari returned after the attack.' He pushes

himself up, and signs to Katvar and me, 'I don't trust these men. We've got you, Micka. We should leave now.'

"Leave" is one of the first sign language words I memorised. Small when spoken, but fussy when signed: your flat palm is facing to the side, then up and down and forward until you close your fist. It takes as long as if you said, 'Discombobulated.'

'You go. I made a deal with them and I'll stick to it,' Katvar answers.

'I'm not leaving you!' My signing is fast and furious. How can he even *think* I would leave him now that we finally found each other again? 'I thought you were dead.'

He shuts his eyes and leans his forehead against mine.

'Fuck, I knew this would happen,' Kioshi blurts out with a groan.

The guy tending to the injured man straightens up and wipes his hands on his shirt. 'Whatever relationship issue you three are having has to wait. We're ready to move.'

KATVAR and I stay shoulder to shoulder, unwilling to let the other out of sight for even a second. And I still can't believe he's here. I've pinched myself a couple of times to make sure I'm not dreaming. I keep scanning his face and clothes, the way he wears his hair like a warrior of ancient times, to make sure it's *really* him. I'd love to hold him, but not now, not yet. We aren't safe. I need to be ready to pull my guns fast and shoot us out if here of need be. Those men who pretend to be BSA? I don't trust them.

I don't trust anyone.

We exit my room, with the badly injured guy carried on a makeshift stretcher behind us. In the corridor, half a dozen men are working on one of the locked doors with a crowbar and a sledgehammer. It gives with a sharp groan of metal.

Someone comes running up the hallway, carrying a first aid kit and a defibrillator. 'Found this in one of the labs,' he calls out and stumbles to a halt. The guys who broke down the door stare through its frame. I can't see what they are seeing, but it can't be good. They shut the door without another word.

Heads swivel toward us.

'You the bitch who killed my men?'

Katvar moves his body in front of mine as I say, 'You the dicks who opened fire on me?'

The guy and Katvar exchange a heavy gaze. I make a mental note to ask Katvar what he told these people about me. I hope he didn't mention that "Bringer of Good Tidings" tale.

The man clears his throat, but the coldness doesn't leave his eyes. 'We'll talk about that later. You have any more explosives?'

'No. And if I were you, I wouldn't open any more of those doors. Ice Face… Colonel Johansson let slip something about bioweapons. I don't know if he lied, but chances are that whatever is being kept in there is dangerous.'

A man who seems to be the leader of this group give me a stiff nod. 'Guess that explains it.' Addressing his men, he says, 'We're done here. Move to the next level.'

'Can I take a look?' I ask.

'Sure. As long as you don't go in.' He opens the door, and everyone who didn't catch a glance the first time steps around the guy and peeks in.

There's a sealed glass door to an anteroom with four showers and four whole-body suits that trail long, flexible hoses up to the ceiling. A large glass wall with another sealed door connects to a lab behind the anteroom. No one's hiding in there. That, and the sealed room with the suits are sure signs this place isn't one we want to enter.

'What *is* this?' someone asks.

Unsure if the question is directed at me, I turn. But the guy who opened the door says, 'High-security lab. They are working with something deadly. From the look of it, viruses or bacteria. Definitely not radioactivity. See those shakers over there?'

He gestures at several platforms the size of small tables. They swivel in lazy circles, turning liquids in dozens of miniature beakers standing on top of them.

'Doc said something about virotherapy,' I volunteer.

The guy shrugs. 'It's not what we came for.' He shuts the door and signals for his men to get going. We proceed to the next level, break through the entrance door and find storage rooms that get the pulse of even the hardest-looking man up a few notches.

'We need more men,' the leading guy says, and barks a few commands into his radio.

We screen room after room. Shelves from floor to ceiling are stuffed with packages and bottles of medicine none of us have ever heard of. Someone hollers down the corridor that he's found analysis kits for blood and urine samples. There are even portable laser scanning microscopes and laminar airflow cabinets, he says. I have no idea what he's talking about, but he's so giddy he's about to hug everyone.

Recovering all this will take a lot of time. 'We need hostages. You have any?' I say to the leading guy.

'We took everyone to the mess hall.'

'Even the soldiers and prison guards?'

He lifts a greying eyebrow. 'Prison guards?'

'There's a prison cell. In the basement, I think.' I feel the gentle pressure of Katvar's shoulder against mine.

The leading guy clicks on his radio and talks. No one exchanges names or ranks. They must all know each other's voices, even through the static crackle.

'We found a basement and a single cell,' grates through the radio.

'Ask him what the cell looks like,' I hear myself say.

A grunt sounds from the other end. 'Meathook in the ceiling, a drain in the floor. Blood and shit all over the fucking place. Looks like they butchered a pig in here.'

I manage a nod. 'That's the prison. Did you run into guards or a man with a face that makes you think your balls will freeze off?'

Cackling on the other end. 'We caught him. He's in the mess with the others.'

My skin prickles, and my hands curl to fists. 'That's Johansson. That guy is dangerous. Isolate him. I'm coming down.'

Katvar follows me like a shadow. Questions are burning in his fingers, but I can't talk about that now. Or anytime soon.

From behind us, I hear the radio spewing an angry, 'And who the fuck are *you*?'

Leader Guy answers, 'Grant them access to the mess, and whatever prisoner she wants to interrogate. If she needs assistance, give her a few of our men.' He flips off the radio and shouts along the corridor, 'Ask Johansson what the high-security wing is for.'

I give him a thumbs up, and ask Katvar, 'Do you have a knife I can borrow?'

I'll need two blades for what I have planned.

Twenty-Seven

On the way down, I screech to a halt and grab Katvar. It surprises both of us, this urgent need to make sure we're both alive and there's not the whole world separating us. I bury my nose against his neck and breathe him in. He rakes his fingers through my hair, cradling my head and soaking up the short moment of privacy and togetherness — things we've both missed since...since...

'How long?' I whisper.

'One hundred and ten days,' he rasps.

I grit my teeth. 'Where are we?'

He pulls back a little. 'Finnish territory. Not far from Lake Päijänne.' He signs the last word slowly, letter by letter.

'No idea where that is.'

'About a hundred fifty kilometres north of Helsinki.'

'Huh. Not as far as I thought. For a three-day train ride… If I even *was* on a train for three days.' I feel lost. Can't trust my own senses.

'You were. We followed you. The two Sequencers who took you left a clear trail in the snow.'

'How? And…why? You were out cold.' I touch my fingers to the thick scar on the side of his head, and my other hand to the other side, where a small pink dot is buried in his shorn hair. Had the small hole the physicians drilled into his skull healed shut completely? Or would the bone never fuse?

'How do you feel?'

A grin spreads over his face. 'Good,' he croaks. And draws his flat hand from his chin toward me. *Thank you.*

'For what?'

'For not giving up,' he signs.

I squeeze my eyes shut. I don't even want to think of those horrible hours in the ice and snow when I thought I'd lost him.

'The cell that man mentioned, was it—'

Gripping his hands, I cut him off. 'Not now. Not…*here.*'

He nods, and brushes a kiss to my brow. I stretch up and press my mouth to his, breathe him, taste him, and feel my heart and my eyes burn.

As we make our way to the mess, Katvar explains the moves of Alta's civil defence — these same guys who are now pretending to be the BSA. They radioed the Sequencers to pick us up right after our plane touched down in Alta. At that point, Alta believed what I'd told them: that we were Ben and Sandra, an injured Sequencer and his apprentice. Then the Sequencers showed up and *arrested* me. And this promised great spoils:

Alta hoped the Sequencers would take me to one of their secret military compounds. They planned to track my movement to find the compound, and then raid it for guns, ammo, and medical supplies. Two of their men on skis followed Mike, Blondie, and me to the rail line, then sent word back via messenger pigeon. The two stayed to observe while they waited for further instructions or reinforcements.

In the meantime, Alta kept looking after Katvar, intending to press information from him once he woke up, perhaps hoping to sell him later to either the Sequencers or the BSA.

By the time the messenger pigeons arrived in Alta, Katvar had regained consciousness. He communicated in writing what he needed to say, and was able to strike a deal with Alta (I still have to dig the details of *that* out of him). Then he and a pilot followed the rail line with our solar plane until they spotted the moving train. They followed it to this base, and the target for this raiding party was fixed.

Katvar's hasty explanation leaves me with even more questions, like how Kioshi ended up here, and why it took more than three months to attack. But there's no time to ask.

A large door to the mess stands open, guarded by two men with assault rifles. 'What took you so long?' one of them asks and waves us in.

'How come the Sequencers didn't ask for their plane back?' I sign to Katvar.

'Because it crashed and burned, and Alta almost lost a man during the rescue mission.'

I snort. 'And they believed that crap?'

Katvar shrugs. I scan the people in the hall. Most are sitting with their backs propped against a wall, their hands tied behind their backs. Some are lying face down on the floor. Chairs and tables have been moved aside and dumped into piles of stiff legs and backrests.

I turn to the guys by the door and whisper, 'The BSA would blindfold the prisoners to disorient them. Do that. And separate the men from the women. Tell them the women are going to be raped, and the men shot. When you leave, pretend you're having to do it in a hurry. You need an explanation for why rapes and executions didn't happen here.' I stop myself and narrow my eyes at them. 'Or don't you?'

Scowling, he scans my reindeer cardigan. The grip on his rifle tightens as he mouths, *Fuck off*.

I wink, put my gun to his face, and bark for everyone to hear, 'Thanks for coming to my rescue guys, but I'm your commanding officer now, in case you didn't notice. Vandemeer isn't here to kick your asses, so it's *me* kicking your asses, whether you like it or not.' I pull my second gun and swivel it toward the bunch of "BSA" guys guarding the hostages. 'Anyone got a problem with that?'

No one says a word.

'Good. Because no one gives a fuck about your feelings anyway, not even your mom. Now, get your pimply asses moving and blindfold these prisoners. Separate the women. And know this: I'll drop a bullet into the ballsack of any man that so much as *thinks* rape.' A wave of relieved sighs runs through the prisoners. The "BSA" guys don't twitch a muscle. They really need to practice up on their look of utter disgust for a woman who barks at them and who's done the unthinkable: forbidden them from raping anyone.

Showing my incisors, I add, 'You can do whatever you want with the bitches when we're back at camp.'

Whimpering makes the rounds. Still, none of the men in black makes to follow my commands. I fire a round at the ceiling. 'Move! Now! And get me some fucking clothes!' That finally gets them going.

I point at two men and send them to fetch the guy with the radio. He comes over with a swagger. 'I hope that helps your authenticity,' I whisper.

He produces a small nod, but his expression doesn't show how he feels about me taking over his show, even if only for a minute.

'I need to find Colonel Johansson and his brother. Johannson's a tall, cold-looking guy with yellow hair, and the other's a doctor with black skin. And there's a woman named Maura, but I'm not sure if she's stationed here.'

'We have the men. Don't know about the woman, though. You going to interrogate them?'

I nod. 'I suspect Colonel Johansson is part of the Sequencer's Espionage Unit. He mentioned bioweapons. Whatever I can squeeze out of him will be useful. Anything you want me to ask him?'

'Locations of other bases. Anything they know about BSA movements. Anything the Sequencers or the BSA have planned for our home territory.'

'I'll do my best,' I answer. 'Can I borrow four of your men? I need tough-looking guys to move my prisoners to the cell in the basement. Push them around a bit, draw a little blood. Nothing too dramatic, though.'

He considers that for a while.

Katvar stands silently by my side, his attention stuck on the prisoners being blindfolded one by one, some of them crying and terrified.

I have no time to feel sorry for the women. Nothing is going to happen to them. Gang rape isn't something I wish on anybody. Yet here I am, inflicting precisely that fear.

Four men are called over to us. Tall, bulky guys with ragged beards and glittering eyes. They receive their instructions and move out. Doc and Ice Face are yanked to their feet and dragged out of the hall. Katvar and I begin to comb through the hostages in search of Maura.

'Where are the soldiers?' my fingers ask Katvar. 'Most of these people here are staff. I've seen some of them in the lab wing.'

'In the barracks.' He tilts his head in the direction Doc and Ice Face were taken, lifts his hands to ask a question, but drops them when I shake my head no.

We step over hogtied and blindfolded people, who jerk as we brush by them.

Every once in a while, I stop my search to sign questions to Katvar. 'How many troops did Alta send? Men to guard these hostages, the ones in the barracks, men to search the labs, to guard the soldiers, that must be…four, or five dozen at least.'

'The soldiers here are all dead.' Katvar's gaze rests on mine, analysing my reaction. But I find I have none. This world is littered with corpses. One gets used to it. Or not.

'Effective,' I say, then sign, 'I want you to stay in the mess hall when I interrogate Doc and Ice Face.'

'No,' he rasps.

I walk faster, digging through blindfolds, but find no Maura. Shit. The woman knows stuff, and I need her in that cell. I want to see her face when she's pushed into my concrete box.

Katvar touches my elbow. 'I am not leaving you alone with this.'

I scrape my hands across my face, and sign, 'This isn't a romantic trip, Katvar. I'm going to *torture* at least one man. Both, most likely.'

His nostrils flare as he puts his face close to mine, then draws back to sign, his fingers slashing the air with determination, 'Do what you have to do. But I will *not* leave you alone.'

I cut back at him, 'I don't want you to see this cell. It is… And I don't want you to see me as…as a monster.'

His gaze softens, his stance does not. 'I see all of you, my love.'

Twenty Eight

Someone's offered me a sweaty shirt, pants that reach past my toes, and a pair of sturdy boots — all taken off some hostages. The boots are perfect, but I left the shirt and the pants with their owners. I'm glad I kept my ridiculous reindeer cardigan because the air is growing chilly on the way to the basement.

One of the bulky men who brought the two prisoners to my cell leads Katvar and me down there. I couldn't have found it on my own. I was blindfolded on the way in, and beaten unconscious on the way out.

Making myself go back to the hospital room is one thing, but this... This lacks all comparison. Every single step down goes against my very nature. My survival instinct is kicking in, my legs want to run the other way. Acid fills my mouth and my heart is racing away from me.

My skin is jittering on my bones.

The stench of dried blood and excrement intensifies, making me gag when we reach a metal door at the end of a corridor. I throw a glance through a peephole. Ice Face and Doc sit at a table that's been brought down from the mess hall. They are looking a bit battered around the nose.

'You've shackled their hands and feet to the chairs?' I ask the guy behind me.

'Eventually,' he says with a smirk, and holds out a small key for their handcuffs.

'You planning to stand guard?'

He nods.

'Thanks. There'll be…noises, but don't come rushing in without looking through the peephole.'

'You think I'm an amateur?'

'No, but you might think *I am*.' I turn to Katvar and sign, 'Are you sure?'

He inclines his head.

A knot forms in my throat. I touch his arm, and then sign, 'Never approach the prisoners with your weapons on you. I'll start with Ice Face. Observe the other guy. I need to know what he's thinking. And if you can't stand it, it's okay to leave.'

'I am not leaving you,' he answers, jaw and shoulders set.

I scan his face. Eyes the colour of pine bark. A severe mouth capable of the softest kisses. 'When we are far away from here,' I whisper, 'Can we try the blueberries and the reindeer milk again?'

Bewildered, he blinks. A moment later, understanding sinks in. His nostrils flare as his gaze flicks to the peephole. There's murder in his eyes.

Hardening myself, I turn away, throw the bolt aside and step back into hell.

With a smile, I greet Ice Face. 'And so we meet again.'

His only answer is a small nod and a curling of his lips, as if to say, 'See, I was right all along.'

I tip my head at Katvar, 'Hand me your weapons, then move the black guy away from the table.' And to Doc, 'I will get to you shortly.'

Katvar moves like the hunter he is: flipping his weapons and handing them to me in one smooth move, grabbing Doc and his chair and sliding him to the back wall, where Doc can see everything but won't be able to interfere even if he throws himself and his chair forward. He'd probably knock himself out on the edge of the table if he tried anything.

Silently, Katvar asks for his knife and gun back, as though we know each other only as commander and soldier. His eyes betray how hard this is on him. He's never witnessed or experienced torture, and now the ugly evidence is punching him in the gut: the clotted gore that covers the floor and splatters the walls. The rusty colours of a variety of dried bodily fluids. This is where the woman he loves was made to bleed and suffer. Where a bunch of men, who believed they were serving the greater good, stole her word-flavours.

Maybe he thinks he won't mind when I retaliate. But something tells me he has no clue what's to come.

Slowly, I pace around Ice Face, scanning the shackles on his ankles and wrists. He's unable to shuffle his feet, but there's enough chain length for him to move his palms up onto the table. Ice Face twists his neck to keep me in his line of sight. One of his eyes has caught a good punch; the lid hangs at half-mast.

When I'm behind him, I switch my gun to my left hand, and my knife to the right. Doc cries out a warning.

Moving fast, I hop up on the table, and stick my gun into Ice Face's visage. 'Open up.'

He ogles me along the barrel, unsure what I want from him.

Crouching low, I snarl, 'I can open your mouth for you, or you do it all by yourself. Your choice.'

His eyes flare in a confusion of rage and terror, but he snaps his mouth open. His chin trembles.

I push the muzzle in deep, then in a bit farther until I hit the back of his throat. His face reddens as he gags on the gun.

'Right hand on the table.'

The chain clinks as he slides his palm onto the tabletop. In a flash, I ram my knife into the back of his hand, driving it through his flesh and into the wood below. His howl pushes around the gun and echoes through the cell. The guy outside scrapes the cover of the peephole aside and coughs, but otherwise remains quiet. Behind me, Katvar doesn't move at all. Or if he does, he's silent. I'm glad he can't see my face and I can't see his.

'Problems breathing?' I ask Ice Face.

His watering eyes are answer enough, but I wait until he produces a tiny nod.

'Would you like me to remove the gun from your mouth?'

Another small nod.

'As soon as you move your hand, the gun will be back, shoved a little farther down your throat. Can you manage not to move your hand?'

He nods again.

'Good boy,' I say, pull back, and push myself up. Ice Face's expression is that of utter relief until I lift my foot and drive the knife deep into the table with a stomp of my boot.

His other hand comes up in an attempt to cradle the injured one, or maybe to rip out the knife.

Holding my hand out to Katvar, I say, 'Looks like I'll need your knife, soldier.'

All blood drains from Ice Face's visage. Even his eyes are paling. His good hand drops under the table.

'I thought so.' I crouch back down, casually dangling the fresh knife and my gun between my knees. 'You see, I'm one of the nice gals. I'm giving you choices. It's all up to you what happens next. Don't you agree?'

He's about to shake his head no, but pulls himself together fast enough and nods.

'*Good* boy.' I gift him a maniac smile. His skin is greying, and his temples are pebbling with sweat.

'Are you in pain?' I ask softly.

'Y-yes.'

'Do you want more of it, or do you want less?'

'Less, pl—' He bites his tongue before *please* can slip out.

I smile. 'So we understand each other.'

He nods.

'Tell me about the high-security labs.'

He doesn't want to, I see it in the flattening of his lips.

I give him a moment to reconsider as I slowly place the mouth of my gun onto the tip of his perfectly manicured index finger. 'Shall I solve your fingernail clipping problem for you?'

'No!' he gasps. 'I'm not involved in the research—'

'One...'

'I'm telling you the truth! I'm not inv—'

'Two...'

His free hand creeps up on the table top. In a flash, I strike with Katvar's knife, push myself up and slam my heel down on its handle.

With a screech, he collapses and hits his forehead on the edge of the table. His chest is heaving. The scent of warm urine wafts through the cell, mingling with the stink of my dried blood and shit.

I wait until he's stopped heaving. 'Are you calm now?'

He nods, lifting his head in small increments. Blood and snot are smeared over his cheek and forehead. The arrogance is wiped clean off.

'Tell me about the high-security labs,' I repeat, keeping my voice gentle and soft. Erik has taught me that. The carrot and the stick work even under torture, or *especially* then. When your prisoner doesn't give you what you demand of him, you strike hard, without delay, without mercy. But when he obeys, you reward him with kind words and some lessening of his pain. Or at least by not increasing it. Erik was fascinated by the way such treatment would always result in an attachment of the tortured to the torturer. I find it one of the most disgusting of human traits. And that's why I drive my teeth into the inside of my cheek when Ice Face looks up at me with a glint of admiration in his eyes. There's also revulsion. A lot of it.

'As I said,' he croaks. 'I am not—'

The mouth of my gun is back on his index finger. 'One.'

He squeezes his eyes shut. That fleeting bit of approval must have come from somewhere else. Maybe he was just acknowledging that when it comes to torture, he can learn from me. Or maybe he's just the mad shithead he is.

'Two.'

The cell is silent except for Ice Face's choppy breathing.

'Three.' The shot cuts through the stillness, bouncing

off the concrete walls. Its echo drowns in Ice Face's and Doc's shouts of pain and shock.

I throw a quick glance under the table to make sure I didn't put a hole in his leg. Nicking a large artery would end this much too soon.

Except for his wet crotch, Ice Face's lower half looks fine.

'He didn't lie! He's not involved in the research!' Doc bellows. 'We grow cell cultures to test our virotherapy agents. We are developing cures!'

'Cut the noise!' I bark.

Ice Face hiccups like a child. Doc keeps insisting they have only humanity's best interest in mind.

'I said: *Cut. The. Noise.*' When nothing happens, I press the muzzle on Ice Face's middle finger and say, 'One.'

That shuts them up immediately.

'Thank you. Now, help me understand this. Are you trying to convince me that only absolutely harmless experiments are conducted in your high-security labs? Is that it?'

'Yes,' Ice Face says.

I nod, hop down from the table, and open the door. Burly Guy looks unimpressed by my interrogation skills. I shake my head imperceptibly at him, then shift my gaze away to talk to a guy who does not exist. 'Go fetch a handful of prisoners — the ones in white coats — and take them to one of the high-security labs. Push them through both sealed glass doors, fire a few rounds at those funny revolving glass thingies, then lock the doors tight and watch what happens.' I step back and shut the door.

'Noooo! You can't do that! Tens of thousands are going to die!' Doc's voice is raw from shouting. A ribbon of spit is stuck to his chin.

I bark a laugh. 'Dude, are you trying to convince the BSA's second in command not to kill tens of thousands?'

'Yes! You are a human being. You are a *woman*. Don't you care about the fate—'

'Oh shut the fuck up!' I cover the short distance to Doc, grab his head and smash his face into the wall. 'Do you know what this is? Do you? It's my blood, my sweat, and the shit and piss your brother beat out of me.'

'I didn't approve,' he croaks.

Disgusted, I step away from him. 'Actually, you *did*. You gave the approval of a coward. You watched it happen. You did nothing to stop it. And then you *partook*. It was your drug your brother *and you* gave me. *You* committed torture. I found no regret in your eyes when you did it.'

'I'm not proud of what—'

'And that is the only reason why you still have a chance, a very small one, to leave this cell alive. Don't fuck it up, Doc.'

He sags in his chair. His head hangs low between his shoulders as he stammers, 'If you would, please, call back your man? So much depends on those cultures.'

I cross my arms over my chest. 'Say "please" again.'

He looks up, eyes watery and pleading. 'Please.'

'I think I might be able to do that for you. But there's a price to pay.'

'Anything you want.' As Doc blurts that out, Ice Face groans and shakes his head. He seems to have forgotten his pinned hands for a moment.

I count my breaths. That's all I can do not to shoot the two of them point blank. The fucks are creating bioweapons, and they *still* believe they are the good guys. 'I want the specifics. Storage locations and volumes. Locations of all the labs and hospitals involved in your research and testing. And I want numbers on the mortality and morbidity of each agent.' I almost whoop when I find the correct terms for this, sounding like an expert. But that's

Runner's training. He taught me about the Great Pandemics, and how tuberculosis and antibiotic resistance are still causing a lot of deaths. But the BSA is the much bigger problem. Until now, that is. *Now* we have the "good" Sequencers cooking up a deadly soup of bacteria to spread…uh…where precisely?

'And I need to know your intended targets.'

Doc looks at me like I'm not speaking English. 'I don't…I don't know what…'

A growl slips up my throat. I point my gun at Ice Face's middle finger, and start counting. 'One…'

'I have no idea what you are talking about!' Doc cries out.

Behind me, Katvar clears his throat. I throw a glance over my shoulder to catch him sign one word at me, 'Truth.'

So Doc has no clue that his brother is dabbling in biowarfare? Interesting.

'Call that man back. *Please!*' Doc's eyes are rolling with panic. 'He's going to destroy decades of research. We'll never be able to start over. We don't *have* the resources. These are the only copies. I'm begging you… I would beg on my knees, but…'

'You're begging me not to destroy your fucking bioweapons? Are you insane?'

Doc's mouth opens and snaps shut with a click. 'W-what?'

'Your brother blabbed about it during one of his torture sessions.'

Doc throws a nonplussed stare at Ice Face. 'Why the bloody hell would you say that?'

Ice Face shrugs. 'She mentioned it, and I played along. You know how it works.'

'How what works?' Doc asks.

'How an interrogation works.' He's white as a sheet. The bleeding has slowed, but the pain must be exquisite.

I flick my finger against one of the knife handles sticking out of his hand. He whinnies like a pony.

'I never got the impression that you knew what you were doing,' I tell Ice Face. 'You were enjoying yourself too much to be productive.'

I hop back up on the table; Ice Face retches as it shivers under my boots. 'The problem is that I don't believe a word. Why the high-security labs if all you are producing is a cure and not a weapon? Why would you want to protect yourself with whole body suits if the stuff you're working on wasn't deadly?'

'We aren't protecting ourselves, we're *protecting the cultures*! For years we had recurring problems with contamination. You see, the cultures are slow growing, which means that just one contaminant can overgrow a test batch in a matter of days. But a few months…no, more than a year ago, we found a high-security lab half buried in the mountains. In Switzerland. We salvaged a lot of the equipment and set it up here. I swear, the suits, the dust-free environment, all of it is to protect our cultures.'

'So if I told you to take a spoonful of each of those cultures and mix them in a glass of water, you and your brother wouldn't mind drinking it?'

Twenty-Nine

It took some throat clearing and cryptic staring at his brother, but eventually Doc nodded agreement. He's on his way up to the lab right now, guard in tow. I don't know what to think of it, or how long he'll be gone. But I'm going to use that time on Ice Face.

He won't be leaving this room alive.

'Tell me about Maura.'

'She's a member of the Council. She was sent here to watch our progress with you, and report back to them.'

'They know about your methods?'

'Yes.'

'How long have the Sequencers been torturing prisoners?'

He stares at this hands, at the hardened rivulets of

blood trailing down his ashen skin, and mumbles something I don't understand.

I place the mouth of my gun against his right middle finger.

'Since the Council was founded!' he shouts in panic.

And I didn't even say, 'One.'

Should it surprise me that the Sequencers have used torture for decades? It probably shouldn't. 'Where do you keep your prisoners of war?'

'Complexes like this one. Small, easy to control and keep hidden, with no more than a half dozen cells.'

I nod, pretending to be satisfied. 'When did you first meet Erik Vandemeer?'

He rears back and accidentally tugs on his hands. Sweat pours from his neck and face as he retches into his lap. When he takes too long getting his heaving under control, I set the muzzle back atop his middle finger. 'One...'

He whimpers. His breath comes in *hap-hap-haps*.

'Two...'

He shakes his head. I'm not waiting for "three." I squeeze the trigger. His roar cuts through the cell, and that's when I sense a faint brush of empathy for him. The feeling disappears in a heartbeat.

'When he... Before he...' Ice Face can't get a clear sentence out. His mouth and throat are working on small chunks of air. His legs are trembling so hard, his knees keep knocking against the table.

'Deep breath in. Deep breath out,' I say softly. 'Come on, you can do it. Deep breath in. And...deep breath out.'

He's breathing now, getting a grip on himself. The trembling doesn't cease though. 'I met him...I don't know...five or six years ago when he was in training for an undercover job.'

So that would explain Erik's first disappearance. Those Sequencers who weren't involved in the Espionage Unit were unable to explain where Erik had gone. Strange that the Espionage Unit hadn't provided a cover story. 'Which undercover job was he given?'

'We never knew who was assigned which job. It's normal procedure. I swear. To protect the missions.'

'Where did you meet him?'

'I will not give away locations. Lives depend on it.'

I pull up Doc's chair and sit close to Ice Face. 'Are you sure?'

His eyes tremble in their sockets, but he manages a nod.

'All right. But you have to give me something else. Two *big* something elses.'

Another nod. He really thinks I'm letting it go.

And I do. For now. 'Number one: Maura. She knows a hell of a lot about that battle on Taiwan, yet she seemed to have no clue I was abducted. Someone fed her intel. You have an undercover agent high up in the ranks of the BSA. Who?'

'We... We were recruiting someone. But he was killed on Taiwan before we could make a deal.'

'Who told you I was working with Vandemeer? Who told you that Erik and I and two of his men escaped Taiwan? Who told you I helped destroy several Sequencer bases? Who told you I destroyed the satellite network. *Who?*' I place the muzzle flat against the base of his pinkie. If fire the shot will rip deep into his hand.

'We don't know!' he cries out. 'After the Taiwan battle, someone at BSA headquarters contacted us. Said he wanted to work for us. He sent us messages, copies of communications between Vandemeer and his second in command, footage of you and Vandemeer directing an attack on our bases.'

'Did that person happen to give you anything useful? Anything that would enable you to save lives?'

'Sometimes, yes. But he wasn't high up enough to be involved in their planning.'

'And you never wondered why he was present when Erik and I led an attack? A man who wasn't ranked high enough to know about attacks well in advance?'

'We did wonder. We thought that maybe...maybe it was a woman. Maybe it was Vandemeer's wife.'

I burst out laughing. 'A regular woman in the command centre? You thought Erik would allow his wife to walk in on his...oh, my. You guys have no fucking clue. He led you around, and you never noticed. Erik has no wife. When he's in heat, he drags a young, untouched girl into his hut. When he and I led an attack on your bases, no one else was in the control room. *He* sent you those messages. *He* had control over your satellites, and let you see and hear want he wanted you to see and hear. Erik fed you the Svalbard footage so that you would come running and cut off my escape route for him. You were his Plan B. He had me rigged and wanted to blow me up. And when that didn't work out, the Sequencers were called in to do the dirty work. But that didn't work out either, because I shot them.'

Ice Face digests my words. His Adam's apple bounces. 'But those men...upstairs...you told those men upstairs you're second in command.' He's growing smaller by the moment. All those layers he's put on to become the tough guy strip away, leaving very little of the person.

'They aren't the BSA. They are people from Alta who need medical supplies, weapons and ammo because the Sequencers stopped offering help. Everything I told you under torture was true. I never belonged to the BSA. I was their prisoner for two years and did what I was forced to do.'

'Why are you—'

'Telling you this? What do you think?

He swallows and blinks. His eyes are leaking. 'You're going to kill me.' A resigned nod, and then, 'Many of us… are trying. We're trying.'

That he isn't begging for his life surprises me. 'Your intentions don't matter. The founding Sequencers vowed to protect humanity. You, your Council, your Espionage Unit, and even your brother abused and broke that vow. You use it as a slogan, nothing more.' Thinking of the amount of medicine they've stockpiled in this building, just because they *could*, makes my trigger finger itch with fury.

'Spare this place. The scientists and my brother.' It's a hoarse whisper he produces. As if his voice is already on its way to a crematory.

'You don't get to tell me what I can or can't do,' I bite out.

Footfalls approach through the corridor. I ask Katvar to signal to them to wait, then turn back to Ice Face. 'Do you think you have the right to ask me not to burn this place to the ground? This place where I was imprisoned, abused, and tortured for months? Treated worse than a dog every minute of the day? By you and your men? Do you?'

'I… No.' He's bared now, stripped of all hope.

'But I will. I am going spare this place, and I'm only doing it because help for my people might come from it one day. There's one condition, though. You will give me the locations of all the Sequencer and BSA bases, all your planned movements in the northern territory. You will give me the specifics on your means of communication and transportation, and the location of the Council. You will tell me everything we need to know to bring the BSA to their knees and to weed out corruption among the Sequencers. And you will spill your guts about your bioweapons. Your brother might not know about them, but *you* do.'

And he talks.

He knows these are the last things he gets to say.

Thirty

Burly Guy is standing by the cell door, his grip a vice on Doc's elbow.

Doc is the last person I want to see right now. His fingers are wrapped around a beaker, the liquid within sloshing against the glass. He must have heard the final shot. And yet, sidling up to the terror in his gaze is a dash of hope. 'My brother. Is he...'

'A worthless piece of shit? Yes.' I pull off my cardigan and use it to rub blood splatter off my hands, then lift my chin at Burly. 'Take him to the mess hall for now. We'll be up there in a minute.'

Doc's movements are mechanical. Stiff. He doesn't fight Burly when he's turned around and nudged toward the narrow flight of stairs that leads up to ground level.

Numb, I watch them disappear. The show isn't over

yet. I still have to make everyone believe that Ice Face kept his mouth shut to the very end.

Katvar is pressing his forehead against a wall, struggling for breath. I sink to the floor and shut my eyes, feeling like a jumble of disconnected joints, aged beyond years. 'I want to go home,' I hear myself say. But where and what *is* home? A safe place? Is any place safe these days?

Grief is suffocating me. I hear myself sobbing, but feel disconnected from the actual thing. Whatever my face and chest are doing, I have no say in it.

Katvar drops to the ground and arcs his body over mine, pressing me to him with what seems to be cries of… of…goodbye? I draw back and look him in the eye. What I see is killing me: Regret. Shame.

He's seen my monster fully formed, and now he knows. Now he *knows*. And he can't bear it.

I scrape my hands over my face, and push myself up. 'Right. Let's finish this.' And I'm not sure if I mean *this job*, or us.

Or myself.

I FIND a bathroom and stare into the mirror. I haven't seen my own face in months. The mirror in my room was only ever interesting as a means of cutting myself free.

The woman I see now is a stranger. Small red droplets mist my face and throat. Black shadows loom under my eyes. My cheekbones are sharper, my jaw harder. My eyes are dead. I don't look like a teenager. I look like the terrorist the Sequencers believe I am. This is what Katvar sees. This is what makes him turn away with regret and shame.

War is riding on your shoulders. A young Lume girl once told me that. It was true then and is even truer now.

I sigh.

I'm not sure I can believe Ice Face's final words as I put the gun to his head. 'I swear we never made them. It was only theory. We never made them.'

Bioweapons. Easy and cheap to manufacture, but hard to deploy if your target is as splintered and fast-moving as the BSA. But the look of fascination in his eyes as he thought of the possibilities... In that short moment, he wasn't even aware of the muzzle pressed to his brow.

My bloody fingers curl around the rim of the sink. Scarlet smears on stainless steel.

I turn on the tap and wash my skin, and can't tear my gaze from the reddened water that circles the drain. Bloody circles. That's what we do. We run in bloody circles of retaliation, chasing our own tails.

DOC IS SQUATTING among a bunch of hogtied and blind-folded scientists, talking to them in a subdued voice. When Katvar and I walk up to them, he has the guts to make demands. 'We'll all drink this if you agree to leave the laboratories untouched.'

I'm so tired of this bullshit, I pull my gun on him. 'My suggestion is that you all drink this, and if it doesn't make you sick, I might only blast off your kneecaps. How's that for a deal?'

He gulps, fumbling for words. 'Please don't destroy this facility. It's going to save lives.'

'Whose? Ours or yours?' I ask, knowing they firmly believe we are BSA.

'Everyone's. Science takes no sides.'

I laugh. 'Is *that* what it is?' I scan the other hostages. 'Take off their blindfolds,' I tell Doc.

He does as asked. Surprised and maybe blinded by the sudden light, Doc's colleagues blink, looking dazed. Until they spot me and my pistol. Instinctively, they duck their heads.

'Science taking no sides,' I say slowly. 'Is that what you did when you watched the abuse of a woman you knew nothing about, and decided to just let it happen? Is that what it was, *not taking sides?*'

I can't believe I wanted to be one of them. And how desperately I wanted it!

Did they too have ideals, honour, and beliefs when they were young, and then…simply forget what once motivated them as they got older? A part of me understands the gradual erosion of one's own values. You grow wiser with age, you tell yourself. But what really happens is that you give less of a fuck because you realise that holding on to your ideals takes a lot more effort than you thought it would.

But maybe these are people who never gave a shit from the start, people who just wanted to be big-brained Sequencer scientists so others would look up to them.

Not really important, though. 'Drink this shit, or I'm going to empty my clip into your bellies, you fucking cowards.' My hate burns white hot, and I love having these people as an outlet. The uproar in my chest has nothing to do with Katvar's reaction to the monster inside me.

Or so I tell myself.

They scramble for the cup and spill a few drops in their haste. I don't care anymore if the concoction kills them, or if they end up dying in twenty or thirty years in their own beds. I just want to get as far away from them as possible.

But I can't. Not yet.

Without glancing at Katvar, I bark, 'Get me a drink, soldier.'

Flashing my teeth at our captives, I turn to find a chair to sit on. A moment later, a cup of cold tea appears in my hand. I look up and find Katvar.

'Thanks,' I mumble, and turn my head away. I can't bear the look in his eyes.

He touches my arm and signs, 'I heard the scientists talking about the stuff in the beaker. They were saying it's tuberculosis bacteria.'

'What? Is the asshole planning to spread that crap around?' I push past Katvar and walk over to Doc to confront him.

'It's a non-virulent strain,' he says, palms up in surrender. The dark patches under his armpits grow bigger every time I talk to him.

Yep, I'm very trigger-happy today. 'Meaning what precisely?'

'These cultures have lost the ability to cause tuberculosis. Or rather, we took that ability away. The bacteria are... um...how can I put it... They are like a farm for bacteriophages, which we hope to use in virotherapy against multiresistant tuberculosis. Drinking this is relatively harmless.'

I stare him down, but he doesn't flinch. Just blinks at me with large puppy eyes.

Okay. He's probably not trying to kill us all. Not today, anyway.

I'm near collapsing, but I straighten my spine, and narrow my eyes at Doc. 'Excellent. As all of you are doing so well, you're ready for a few questions, yes? Colonel Johansson was a tad...how should I say...reticent? I'm sure you can help a lady out. I need the locations of all Sequencer bases in Scandinavia, the location of your Council, your means of communication and transport, access codes, *etcetera etcetera*, and everything you've planned against us. In turn, I won't kill you by carving your limbs from your body. But if you think you might need more convincing, I'll drag you to my pretty cell in the basement and sit you down with Johannson's remains.'

'We don't know anything about strategies against the BSA or locations of secret bases. We are scientists, not soldiers.'

Slowly, I turn my head to the woman who has spoken. She's a head shorter than the others, and there's a fierceness to her that I like.

'I don't see that as a problem, because someone in this mess hall *does* know. So I'll be torturing and killing as many scientists as it takes for that person to come forward.'

She blanches and grabs the arm of the man next to her for support. He barely registers the touch.

I smile at them and say to Doc, 'I'll get to you shortly.'

Then I turn on my heel, jerk my chin at the guy with the radio, and march back to my chair and my cup of tea. A single line is on constant repeat in my head: "need to get out of here need to get out of here."

The man in charge of this group approaches casually, pulls up a chair and plops down on it. Even bumps me with his elbow as if we're chums. 'When you're done with the prisoners, you want us to burn everything to the ground, or leave the labs so we can come back later and get more stuff?' He says it loud enough for Doc and his staff to hear. The whites of their eyes are showing. A couple of them are crying, and I'm not sure if they are concerned about the life and well-being of anything but their fucking bacteria and viruses.

I bend close to Leading Guy's ear and whisper, 'Leave the labs untouched, but act like we're getting ready to blow everything up, including the prisoners. Are we ready to leave now?'

He nods, and clicks the button on his radio four times without saying a word.

I lean back and gift our hostages an ugly sneer. They all sag in despair.

A MINUTE LATER, a bunch of men I haven't seen before come storming in and shout something about enemy movements and that we have to get the fuck out of there. They are so authentic my pulse is jumping until Katvar signals to me that all is going as planned.

Maybe the new ones were on recon while everyone else was inside the building, and were called back in for the pretence of needing to leave in a hurry.

So that's what we do. We exit the building like it's on fire. Night engulfs us. I suck in the fresh air and feel the wetness of tears on my cheeks. I don't mind the couple of mosquitoes I inhale on the way.

My one hundred and ten days of terror are over.

I.

Am.

Free.

I can't fill my body fast enough with all this beauty. The starry sky stretching over us, and a gibbous moon sitting bright in the treetops. The scents of grass, earth, and pine sap. The sounds of insects. A lazy breeze that's shifting balmy air. It is summer and I am free.

Katvar grabs my hand and tugs me along to keep me from falling back too far. I'm exhausted and ridiculously out of shape. Sweat plasters my shirt to my spine, and my sides are aching.

We enter a forest. Thick moss muffles footfalls. Our

troops are splitting up into small factions. I can barely see the shape of the men in this darkness, and then they are gone. It's only Katvar and me now, and the silent trees that flit past us.

Mosquitoes are colliding with my face. I keep my mouth shut and my legs pumping. I can't help thinking back to what Ice Face said about that mysterious BSA guy the Sequencer's Espionage Unit was trying to recruit. If that man was Erik, then my father knew I was on Taiwan before we even found the BSA camp's location. That would allow only one conclusion: Cacho, the old Sequencer who visited my village when I was a kid, must have been Erik's all along. It was Cacho who somehow managed to get Runner to consider me for an apprentice. Runner, who'd never before had an apprentice and hadn't ever planned to have one. How did Cacho manage to convince Runner? And where is Cacho now, if he's still alive?

No, wait. Erik had control over the Sequencer's satellites even then, and could have eavesdropped on any of their conversations. He could have heard that Mickaela Capra was on her way. But that would be too much of a coincidence. Picking my name out of the hundreds of daily Sequencer communications? Not likely.

My mind keeps interfering with my running, and Katvar has to keep tugging on my arm so I don't come to a complete standstill.

Did Runner suspect corruption within the Sequencer Council and Espionage Unit? Was that part of the reason he decided to stay on Taiwan and spread that "Bringer of Good Tidings" tale? I *need* to know. If we still have the solar plane, maybe we can—

Grunting, I bump into Katvar. 'Oompf. Sorry. Didn't realise we were stopping.' Bending over, I press my fists into my aching sides. A cloud of mosquitoes gathers around me. Again Katvar tugs on my hand. He pulls me into some kind of miniature shack, or tries to, because my feet just won't move.

'I'm not going into another box!' My voice comes out squeaky. My nerves are raw and every fibre of me is so fucking done with being cooped up and chased around.

'Mosqu—,' he croaks, but his voice is giving up halfway. He scrambles into the shack and returns with a small oil lamp that stinks so sharply my eyes water when the smoke hits my face. The mosquitoes hate it enough to stay away, though.

He waves me toward a fallen tree, to sit on the mossy side, then places the oil lamp next to me and disappears into the hut once more. The ramshackle thing is more a hole in the ground than an actual building. It's well camouflaged. I bet I'd run past it even in bright daylight.

Katvar clambers back out with a loud huff, enters the small circle of light by my feet, and places food on the forest floor. Bread, smoked meat and fish, even a piece of cheese. I'm hungry, but my stomach is in knots. Now that he and I are finally alone together and silence envelops us, I find I can't face what he has to say. I can't face goodbyes between us.

For a heartbeat, he catches my gaze, then drops his head and sucks in a stuttering breath.

He is in pieces and so am I. The hope that he was alive and that we would see each other again was all that kept me going. And that's all I'm going to get now: him alive and this last meeting between us.

Emptiness yawns inside me. The world is losing all colour. I hear myself whisper, 'Just say it,' because I've always run at my problems head-on, whether I've wanted to or not.

Katvar sinks to his haunches and presses a hand over his mouth. His eyes are blazing in pain with all the things he can't seem to bring himself to say.

'It's okay.' Tears are choking me. 'I understand.'

He shakes his head and lifts his hands. His signs — which usually translate themselves fluidly into sentences in my head — make no sense to me at all. 'Now I fail you. Before I fail you. Next I fail you.' He crashes a fist against his chest. 'I fail you. Again, again, again.'

He thinks that to leave me is to fail me?

'I don't hold you to your promises.' Where do I even get the strength to say these words? Love. From my love for him. I can't bind him to me when he can't even look at me without regret and shame. 'You are not failing me. If anything, I've failed you. You don't have to love what's become of me.'

'What?' he croaks, and lifts his gaze.

'I'm not good for you, Katvar.' Why can't my fucking tear ducts shut up and let me say my thing? My voice is warbling and I'm suffocating on pain. 'It's okay. I understand. You saw what I did. What I *am*. And I... I keep taking from you. Keep making you do things that—'

He cuts me off with a gentle hand to my lips, then signs, 'I don't know what you mean. You want me to leave?'

I can't hold it in any longer. My face screws up as sobs burst from my mouth. 'No, no, I don't want you to leave. But I understand that you don't want me anymore.'

I tip forward, and he grabs my shoulders, lets me cry my grief against his chest.

'I am not enough,' he rasps.

'You are *everything*.'

His arms contract around me. He's crushing me to

him, but to me, it feels like he's letting go, not holding on to me. To us.

Bracing himself, he gently pushes me away, and signs, 'Micka, I nearly got us both killed on Bear Island. You had to drag me out of there and find a doctor. And *that* got you arrested, and…tortured. For one hundred and ten days I *knew* where you were. Runner would have got you out immediately. All *I* did was wait. If I can't protect you, how will I ever be able to protect our family?'

Before he can continue, I snatch his hands in mine. 'Aren't you disgusted by what you saw me do? What I'm capable of? Don't you want to…to run away from me?'

He shakes his head and squeezes the living daylights out of my fingers.

'You are not shocked that I tortured a man? I executed that guy!'

He pulls my knuckles to his lips, then lets go of my hand to sign, 'No. What I saw in that cell… The blood. *Your* blood. I wanted him to suffer. To suffer more. I watched you take your revenge and press information from him, and I wished it was me, me who put that bullet in his head.'

I know it's the wrong moment to whoop with joy, but I could totally… Oops! Did already. 'And you…you think you've failed me because a bunch of assholes locked me up?'

He nods, jaw clenched.

I want to throw my arms around him and laugh, shake him and tell him none of this was his fault. But that won't be enough. I've blamed myself for Runner's death so many times. And just because I don't want Katvar to suffer the same way, doesn't mean I can wipe away his feelings of guilt with a laugh and a clap to his shoulder.

'Did you or anyone from Alta's civil defence suspect the

Sequencers would torture me?' I know the answer, but I want *him* to say it.

He squeezes his eyes shut and shakes his head no.

'What was the aim of the mission today? To get in and out with minimum losses? Or was it to blow everyone to pieces?'

His fingers slash at the air. 'That's not the point!'

'It is the *whole* point! How do you think I'd feel if you'd blasted your way in, got dozens of your own troops killed, and ended up dead before you even reached me? I'm just one person. No one should risk the lives of many for the life of one!'

He keeps shaking his head. I touch his cheek, and whisper, 'I don't need you to kill people for me. I don't *want* you to kill people for me. Just love me. That's all I need.'

Thirty-One

There's so much doubt and pain in Katvar's eyes, it breaks my heart all over again. I need him to be all right. And I need to dull our pain and just *feel* him. Nothing else. Just him.

I lean into him and slant my mouth over his. It's not gentle. It's ravenous, greedy, ruthless. He opens for me, claws my back, my head, my thighs and tries to wrap all of me around all of him. His moans feather across my neck as his hands slip under my shirt to burn skin that's been cold with loneliness for one hundred and ten days. He trails kisses along my jaw, and…jerks back.

'Are you okay?' I whisper as he snatches the stinky lamp and holds it up to my face.

'Wound,' he croaks, and scans my neck with the rough pads of his fingertips. Frowning, he pulls the collar of my shirt down to my shoulder and runs his thumb over my skin.

With a huff he sits back and signs, 'Not yours.'

'Not mine what?' My hand flies up to my neck and finds a crust of blood. Can only be Ice Face's. Maybe even brain matter. 'Ew!'

Shuddering, I rub my palm over the moss.

He nods. 'Let's go for a swim. There's a lake that isn't far, and we shouldn't stay here much longer anyway. And...I have something for you.' Katvar disappears into the small, half-buried hut.

I collect our food and the stinky lamp, and follow him. Lifting the hatch, I peek inside, but all I can see is the searching beam of a squeeze light and Katvar's outline in the cramped space.

'What's this thing? Did you build it?' I ask.

I forget my question when I see what he's carrying as he pushes back out through the door: There's a ruck on his back, and bow and quiver poking over his shoulder. In one hand he holds a second ruck, and in the other...

'My *rifle*? You went back to Bear Island?' Hastily, I place our food back on the forest floor.

He hands me my weapon, and I can't help but wrap my fingers around the cold metal and press it to my chest. As long as I have this, I can protect us.

'The SatPad?' I ask.

He pats the side of his ruck. 'It's here. Let's go.'

Goosebumps skitter down my spine. 'Yes. Let's go.' I stuff the food into my ruck, shoulder my pack, check my rifle, and turn to go.

But he grasps my elbow and turns me back to face him. He just looks at me, scans my face as if to memorise each freckle. 'I missed you,' he signs. With a smile, he leans in, kisses my forehead, and whispers hoarsely, 'Love.'

As he leads the way, I scan our surroundings with my scope's night-eye. Doc or someone else must have radioed for help by now. Which reminds me: 'How did you guys manage to attack without the Sequencers calling for reinforcements? Or...did they?'

He puts the squeeze light between his teeth to sign, 'Alta did something to the radio signals before we attacked. Jamming is what they called it. Neutralising the Sequencers' defence and communication was step one of our attack. Jamming was easy, but taking out the troops was difficult. We had to make sure only the armed guys went down, and that you, the staff, and patients were safe. We thought...it was a hospital where they were keeping you.' His hands grow heavy with guilt as he signs the last sentence.

'That you and Alta managed all that in three months is a feat. You know that, don't you? Did you have help from the inside?'

He waggles his head. 'Sort of. A family of charburners lives nearby. That hut...' He motions at the darkness we came from. '... is one of theirs. They deliver wood and charcoal to the Sequencers. That's how we got the poison in.'

'What? With wood?'

Katvar's teeth flash white in the darkness. 'Twice a week their troops have some major combat training session, and after that, they all sweat in a sauna, then jump into an artificial pool. One of us sneaked in with a charcoal delivery and put poison in the pool water. It made them drowsy and easier to kill.'

It's strange to hear Katvar talk almost casually about killing people. I nod and keep walking, one eye on the scope. The small hairs on my neck are prickling as though someone is hot on our heels. But there are no heat signatures other than Katvar's and mine, and those of small, nocturnal animals. Silently, we head through the woods until a silvery smooth surface peeks through the black trees. The moon's reflection on the lake looks like a giant, off-kilter egg.

We find a mossy place to sit, but I'm on edge. Something's going to happen. Someone's going to find us and drag us back, lock us up, dish out pain.

To distract my taut nerves I ask, 'How did you know they kept me in the lab wing?'

Katvar finishes placing our food on the forest floor, and signs, 'We didn't know which wing or level, just the building. The pilot I came with saw you being dragged into it. We watched the place around the clock, and never saw you exit.'

'Is the radio signal still jammed?'

He shakes his head no. 'The group responsible for making sure the troops were down, and the weapons and ammo located and taken, also took care of radios and other gadgets that can be used for communication. I hope they found SatPads. We have to make copies of our library.'

'What do you mean "took care of radios"? Did they destroy them?'

'The plan was to take what we could carry, and destroy the rest. It's a three-day hike to the next settlement with a radio station.' He touches my knee, motions to me and him, and signs a single word: 'Safe.'

Snorting, I stand, lift the scope of my rifle to my eye and scan our surroundings for heat signatures again. Nothing but small reddish splotches: owls and martens hunting mice.

'*Nowhere* is safe, Katvar.' I glance back at him.

He holds his hand out to me. Such a simple gesture. But even that doesn't make me feel better. It used to, but not anymore.

'I'll walk the perimeter while you eat,' he signs.

Reflexively, I tighten the grip on my rifle. The reaction startles me. I have to force my fingers to uncurl and my arms to offer the weapon to him. He sees the effort it takes for me to let go, but says nothing.

'Hope for the best and prepare for the worst,' I tell him.

He motions at the food. 'Eat. Rest. I'll keep us safe.' And then he leaves.

I EAT the way I've been eating the past one hundred and ten days: hurried and unable to taste what's on my tongue. When Katvar silently returns from recon, he finds me crouched in the underbrush, pistol and knife at the ready. We take a swim in the lake, but I'm wound up tight and don't enjoy a single second of it.

I'm trapped in a shell of fear.

Katvar's brought blankets and a change of clothes for us, and now offers to take first watch so that I might sleep for a few hours. But I can't shut my eyes. I fire question after question at him, digging for details on Alta's strategy. How precisely did they plan the attack? What went according to plan and what didn't? Where did the others go, and how are they going to get back home? Where are *we* going? What's our next step, and the ones after that?

He answers patiently until I run out of questions to ask.

'Trust me?' he signs.

'I do.'

'Why don't you try to sleep, Micka?'

I dig my nails into palms. 'I'm afraid to be unprepared, vulnerable. I'm afraid this is a dream and I'm going to wake up in my cell.'

'Tell me?' The movements of his fingers are soft and flowing.

I open my mouth and pause. Fear of reliving everything makes me hesitate. But not talking about it isn't going to protect me from nightmares either.

And so I tell him about the injections, the shackles, the concrete box, the nail clipping, the spoonfuls of mush thrown on the floor to feed me. The cold showers with a hose. I talk until my throat is raw and my mind is empty.

THE RISING SUN finds me with my head on his lap, and his hand in my hair. Turns out I did sleep after all.

Thirty-Two

My panic has come back with full force. I'm scared of *everything*.

I'm scared the vibrations of our solar plane mean we're going to crash. We're high up and there are no clouds blocking my view of the abyss below. I'm scared that the many boxes of medications, test kits, disposable gloves, medical tools, bandages, and whatnot will shift and crush us, although it's not possible to be crushed by what weighs so little. I'm scared of the pistol strapped to the co-pilot's hip, and of Katvar flying the plane. There are many ways to die, and I am familiar with them all.

Breathing is an effort. My body has known fear for so long that it knows little else. I have to force air in and out of my lungs in long, deep breaths so as not to hyperventilate. My heart is bruising my ribs. My fingers hurt from holding my rifle in a death grip.

As we land in Alta, I'm close to vomiting with terror. The swarm of people rushing at us for the supplies we've brought only makes it worse. Katvar manoeuvres me across the airfield and away from everyone. He finds a place where no one can see us, gently pulls my fingers one by one from my weapon, and wraps his arms around my jittering frame.

I fist his shirt and bite the inside of my cheeks until the metallic taste of blood spreads in my mouth. *Blood*. Yes. That's what's going to fix me.

I drop to the ground, pull off a boot and unwrap the bandage from around my injured ankle. Without looking up at Katvar, I explain in short gasps, 'Gonna cut myself. Need to stop the panic. My chest is going to burst if I don't.'

Maybe he'll hate me for it, be disgusted by me, run away from me. But I can't *not* cut my skin now. The breathless split second before death is hitting me — that's precisely how I feel right now. The cold, logical part of my mind knows I'm safe, but the rest of it and all of my body firmly believe I'm going to die. Now. But as there is no danger to run from and no enemy to attack, my system is thrown into chaos and blind terror.

Calmly, Katvar sits down and wraps my bare foot in his warm hands. Without flinching he lets me do what I need to do. One, two, three. Four incisions. The sharp pain stitches me back together. I watch as thin ribbons of blood trickle onto the earth and are swallowed by it. My chest relaxes. My throat is finally able to let air through. Sighing, I sink down onto my back and breathe. A flotilla of clouds rides on winds high up in the sky. Cries of an eagle sound from afar.

Katvar bandages my ankle, pulls on my sock, puts my boot back on and laces it. He lies down next to me and entwines his fingers with mine. Together, we watch the clouds until he points up and says hoarsely, 'Dinosaur.'

'Looks like a boar to me.'

'Too long neck.'

'It's the common northern long-necked boar. It was a delicacy until the entire species was fried and eaten. If I remember correctly, it happened in 1974.'

He snorts and turns on his side. His brow is in deep creases as he touches his fingers to my cheek. 'I'm so sorry I wasn't there for you.'

'What they did to me was not your fault. It was their's.'

'Wouldn't you feel the same if it had been me in that cell?'

I smile. 'Yes. And wouldn't you be trying your best to convince me that I'm not responsible for any of it?'

When he smiles back at me, it's as if a second sun rises.

'I completely forgot about Kioshi!' I burst out. 'Where is he? And why the hell was he at the base? Oh, and the dogs? Did you find them?'

'I picked them up when I got our stuff from Bear Island. Left them with the Sami here for the time being. And Kioshi… He was the only one I could think of to help us. He's my best friend and understands my language. Olav — the Pilot who gave me flying lessons — and I searched several of the Lume's summer camps until we found him. Kioshi, I mean.'

Katvar lifts his face to the sun. 'Kioshi must be with the Sami now. He and most of the others were flown in last night. I promised him we'd meet them when we get back, and then talk to the elders.' His gaze slides to the hangar. He swallows. 'Micka, there's a…thing I need to do. Will you stay here and wait for me?'

'What thing?' Something's off, I can feel it.

'The deal I made…' He sits up and rubs his palms over his thighs, and tells me about several favours he asked of Alta, offering them only one thing in return: an electronic library of two million books, half of them in advance, the other half if the mission was successful. He could have demanded the whole city for this treasure but asked only for help to find and retrieve me, to be allowed to keep our solar plane and be taught how to fly it, and to be given enough provisions for a week when we leave.

'But where's the problem?' I ask.

'I'm going over to let them make a copy of the other half now, and then…then there's another small favour, the last one I'm going to call in. But I'm not sure you still want it.'

I roll onto my side and sit up. 'Want what? What favour?'

He curls his hands to fists. A tremor runs through his frame as he exhales, and signs, 'To get screened for genetic defects.'

I puff out a breath I didn't know I was holding. 'Why wouldn't I want that?'

I've been trying to talk him into that for months. He's always wanted to be a dad, but never dared dream of it because he was too afraid of the mark his father left on his genome.

He drops his gaze to his lap. 'Because I didn't protect you.'

That's when I remember the desperate words he spoke last night: *If I can't protect you, how will I ever be able to protect our family?* It hadn't registered then, but now… 'You want babies?'

Half a nod from him is all it takes for me to lunge and wrestle him to the ground. I stare down into his warm, brown eyes. An ear-to-ear smile has me looking pretty stupid right now. 'You want my babies.'

'Badly,' he rasps.

HAND IN HAND, we walk to Alta's hospital to meet the physician who drilled a hole in Katvar's skull. Her name is Bente, she tells me, as she runs a thin metal spatula across the inside of Katvar's cheek, and then holds out a fresh spatula to me.

Puzzled, I draw back.

'Last time I checked, two people are needed to procreate. Open up!' She swabs me and tells us to come back in two hours.

'Uh, I thought it took twelve hours or so to sequence a human genome with an MIT FireScope,' I mutter.

She shrugs. 'There's no need to sequence and analyse the whole genome. Screening for known genetic defects is enough. Takes the machine one and a half hours, and me another ten or twenty minutes to look through the results and make sure they're correct.'

'You're doing a lot of this?'

'Since we got this machine, yes. We can diagnose infections and check for antibiotic resistance, we can screen for inherited disorders. It's extremely useful. Now stop bothering me.' She grins and walks away.

'Is she always like that?' I ask Katvar.

'I think she calls it "humour".'

He leads the way out of the hospital and through the streets of Alta. It looks friendlier now than it did when I last saw it and winter still had a tight grip on the land. The windows are covered with gauze, not reindeer skin. Kids are playing soccer in the streets. A couple of adults argue over who's responsible for fixing a particular stretch of pavement.

Odd. I haven't seen signs of peace for months — years, if I don't count the short time at the Lume's winter quarters — and I learned not to expect it.

All I ever expect is violence and war.

'So the BSA didn't attack Alta after all?' I ask Katvar.

'They disappeared after they lost Tromsø.'

'They'll probably be back.'

'Probably.' He stops walking. 'What about Ice Face? Will you tell them what we know?' He jerks his chin in the direction we're heading.

'No, I… I don't trust these guys. And they don't trust me. I killed four of their men.'

He scans my face. 'You are planning something.'

I open my mouth. Breath dies in my throat. 'I'm going to start a war.'

His eyes darken. 'Micka, no!' he croaks.

Katvar is a pacifist at heart. If he could, he would bring peace to everyone, even to the BSA.

I take a step closer to him and whisper. 'You will like this one, I promise.'

He lifts an eyebrow.

'What if the Sequencers and the BSA were so extremely busy with one another that they had no time to bother anyone else? Doesn't that qualify as peace?'

A frown carves his brow as his gaze begins to drift in thought. He snaps his eyes back at me and signs, 'You'll use Alta's strategy to burn out the BSA and the Sequencers?'

Grinning, I softly bump my fist against his belly. 'I love how your brain works.'

'It's bold, this strategy.'

'You think it will work?'

'If you'd asked me before I saw Alta march into that

Sequencer base and come back out victorious, I'd say, no. But now…I think it might work.'

'You with me in this?'

He hesitates, then gives me a semi-nod.

I nod. 'You're sceptical.'

He shifts his gaze over my shoulder, toward the city centre. Somewhere there is the council house and a handful of Alta's civil defence waiting for us to show up and hand over the other half of our electronic library.

'Who will you ask for help?' he signs.

'People we trust. No more than a dozen. And I'm going to train them.'

He's dead serious when he asks, 'You plan to win a war with a handful of warriors?'

Silently, we hold each other's gaze. There's no need to discuss the extremely high risk of failure for such undertaking. But if we win, the reward will be immense. Neither of us can remember the time before the BSA declared war on the world. This war is older than the remaining 2986th part of ten billion humans. Katvar and I weren't even born then, and neither were our parents or grandparents.

I take his hand in mine and brush my thumb over his knuckles. 'It's time we ended this. I don't want to be another mother who loses her children in a battle some old megalomaniac fart starts.'

He lifts our entwined hands and presses a kiss on my wrist.

'Together,' he whispers across my skin.

THE BALTIC SEA is a deep blue blanket spreading out far below us. I tell myself that if we crash, we can swim. It's bullshit but it's the only thought that keeps my panic at bay.

Fear stirs just under my skin, making my heart jump and my breath come in short bursts.

Katvar is cradling my hand in his lap as he pilots our solar plane. It's his third solo flight, he tells me. I'm not sure if that's supposed to make me feel better.

I scan his beautiful profile and can't believe the devastating news Bente gave him. Katvar carries a gene defect that can cause Roberts Syndrome — one of the rarest of all genetic disorders, according to her. She also told us that we can have as many kids as we want, because Roberts syndrome only manifests if *both* parents are carriers of this mutation, and I am not. The defect is so extremely rare, it occurs in only one of four billion people. He must be the only Roberts Syndrome carrier on this planet.

He was shocked by the news. Partly because he's been right all along: His genetic makeup *is* marred by inbreeding. And partly because I've been right, too: He's healthy, and his kids and grandkids will be just as healthy as other children.

That he now has proof for both rattles him deeply. He can have perfect kids of his own, while not being perfect himself. Maybe it feels to him a bit like his father's wrongdoings are redeemed.

We'll both need time to come to grips with this. With the sudden fortune bestowed on us after all the suffering.

And we've been lucky to leave Alta unharmed. The Sami informed us that Alta's civil defence had planned to keep us for ransom and auction us off to whoever offered the highest bid, the Sequencers or the BSA.

Again it was Runner's tale that saved our lives: The Sami believe Katvar and I have been sent by the Bringer of Good Tidings. They watched the sky burn. Kioshi told them that we did this, that we destroyed the BSA's most important means of reconnaissance and communication.

A simple warning by the Sami — that if we were not allowed to leave untouched, they would never again supply Alta with reindeer meat and furs — was enough to make Alta step back.

THE LEGEND IS SPREADING among the hunter tribes of the North, growing stronger with each passing season. Was that what Runner wanted?

OUR THREE DOGS are leashed to a passenger seat in the back. My rifle is strapped to my ruck on the floor behind me. An unknown future awaits.

END

The final instalment of Micka's and Katvar's adventures is coming soon. Sign up to my newsletter, so you won't miss it.

Acknowledgments

This book wouldn't have happened without a bunch of great and lovely people.

I'm indebted to:

Sebastian Roberts for the most enjoyable discussions on how to best take over the world.

Magnus for loving Micka, and being the first to read everything I write.

Ralf Kleemann, Float Pilot from the Alaska Bush Pilot Forum, and Antares from KBoards for helping me gut Micka's solar plane to get it off the ground.

My faithful readers and friends at silent-witnesses.com for for supporting this project and our small owl rehab: Victoria Dillman, Philip Heather, Gloria Gorton-Young, Therese Webster, Caroline Wolfram, Michael Morrison, Kim Wright, Louis Valentine, Terry Kearns, Debby Avery, Walki Tinkanesh, Steve Howard, Linda Koch, Tom Welch, Gudrun Theater, Carry Pandya, Linda Stepp, and Nancy McDonald.

Tom Welch for being my friend, even though he has to

proofread all my crap, and then proofread it again because I keep tinkering with it.

You, dear reader, for coming back to Micka and Katvar (*I didn't kill him! Yay, me!*)

And Peppa, the best-ever rescue barn owl in the world, for all the affection she so generously bestowed on us, and every minute she spent in our company. We treasure every memory of you, little owl. I hope you find the fattest mice and the loveliest owl partner, and live a long and happy owl life.

Made in the USA
Middletown, DE
03 July 2022